HARD

Hard and Fast

Linda Newbery

ARMADA

Hard and Fast was first published in Armada in 1989.

Armada is an imprint of the Children's Division,
part of the Collins Publishing Group,
8 Grafton Street, London W1X 3LA

One

Several cars were already parked in the driveway of the *Cocked Hat* Restaurant, and the subdued lighting inside cast a warm pink glow on the drawn curtains. Chris led the way round the side of the building, towards the kitchen entrance.

"What's the point?" Lisa asked, stumping awkwardly behind him, her high heels skewing and teetering in the gravel. She stopped and balanced on one racehorse-slim leg, lifting her other foot to examine a scuff on her shoe. She looked round at Gary for sympathy. "I bet Melanie won't want to come anyway," she told him. "Even if she's not working, she's probably doing her homework, or something else just as boring."

Chris walked on regardless. The kitchen door was open, in spite of the chill of the early spring evening, and an aroma of steak and onions and mushrooms wafted out on a hot breeze. "Hi, is Melanie there?" he called.

"Just a sec," called a male voice from within, above the clatter of dishes. After a few moments, a tall girl, with dark springy hair pinned into submission under a white cap, appeared in the doorway. Her large, rather plain face lit with an animated smile as she saw Chris standing outside.

"We're just going to the disco," Chris explained. "Gary, Lisa and me. We came to see if you wanted to come, but you're obviously working. You can't come later on, I suppose?"

"Sorry, no. We've got a lot of bookings tonight, and one of the waitresses is off with 'flu." She wiped her damp hands vigorously on her striped apron. "I've been thinking of fund-raising ideas," she continued eagerly. "And I got some more stuff in the post. I'll tell you all about it on Monday." She turned in response to a shout from inside. "Look, I'd better go back in. Thanks for coming round. I hope you have a good time."

"I told you she wouldn't come," Lisa reminded the two boys as they scrunched across the gravel again. "And honestly, can you imagine her at the disco? Knowing her, she'd probably turn up in something from the Oxfam shop, just to be different."

Gary laughed at this, and Lisa giggled and threw back her blonde curls, secretly glad that she would have Chris to herself for the evening, after all.

In the restaurant kitchen, Melanie returned to her task of chopping and arranging garnishes. She was only half-sorry not to have been able to go out with the others. Discos and parties weren't really her scene, and she didn't like the effort of pretending to be enjoying herself when really she'd rather be *doing* something. Besides, her friendship with Chris hadn't been the same since he'd started going out with Lisa. She'd known Chris since primary school, and they'd been friends for so long that they felt relaxed and easy in each other's company, but Lisa, with her provocative clothes and sharp manner, had changed that. Chris had had girlfriends before, but none of them had seemed quite so intent on gaining a stranglehold over him. Worse, Chris himself seemed to have changed, living up to what Lisa expected of him, trying to act hard and sophisticated in ways Melanie didn't like.

"Perhaps it's just a phase he's going through," Melanie thought, chopping coriander energetically, then grinned at herself, aware that she sounded like her grandmother.

"Can you take over waiting for a minute, love?" Her mother, a smaller and plumper version of Melanie, hurried into the kitchen with a perilously loaded tray. "There's some people just come at table Five."

"Yes, okay." Melanie swapped her striped kitchen apron for a white frilled one, straightened her black skirt, picked up her notebook and pen, and walked round the screen which hid the kitchen door from the diners in the restaurant. As she did so, she assumed the polite half-smile she wore for waitressing, and glanced swiftly around the restaurant.

The new arrivals at table Five, a smart couple and

7

a teenage girl, looked as if they might be ready to order. It was only when she was standing by their table with pen and notepad poised that Melanie realized that the girl was looking up at her with recognition. Melanie looked back. Yes; that barley-coloured, straight, chin-length hair was really quite distinctive – it was just that Melanie wasn't in the habit of scrutinizing customers closely, and besides, the girl looked different out of school uniform. She was Ruth someone – new in Melanie's form at school, and apparently shy.

"Hello," Melanie said, acknowledging Ruth's hesitant smile.

Ruth's parents seemed surprised, looking up at Melanie as if she had spoken out of turn. The woman, who was well-groomed and dressed in understated, elegant clothes, gave the orders briskly: whitebait, pâté, egg mayonnaise, steaks, and a bottle of champagne. Must be a wedding anniversary or birthday, Melanie thought, dismissed. She decided that she didn't envy Ruth her parents; smart, young, obviously well-heeled, rather imperious-looking, especially the mother. Ruth, though, looked as if she might be nice. Melanie made a mental note to approach her about the fund-raising. A wealthy mummy and daddy might be a positive asset. This thought immediately struck Melanie as rather calculating, but then, she told herself, she would need to be calculating if she were to achieve her aim of raising a thousand pounds.

* * *

Ruth ate her egg mayonnaise thoughtfully. She felt embarrassed by the fact that the girl who had taken their order was in her form at school; it seemed all wrong to be sitting there while the girl danced attendance. Ruth squirmed inwardly as her mother beckoned to Melanie and addressed her in the abrasive tone she used when wishing to make her presence felt.

"I did ask for iced water, if it isn't too much trouble."

Melanie's face was impassive, not betraying the irritation which Ruth was sure she must have felt. "Of course – I'll fetch it straight away."

Ruth tried to compensate for her mother's brusqueness by saying "Thank you", as Melanie put the glass jug on the table. But she spoke more loudly than she had intended, so that her words sounded sarcastic.

"Do you know that girl?" her father asked, buttering a roll. "You keep grinning at her."

"She's at my new school," Ruth replied. "In the same form."

'Really?" Her mother was looking round the restaurant in a rather bored way. "You'd think that fifth years would have too much homework and exam preparation to want to work in the evenings."

"A lot of them have Saturday or evening jobs," Ruth said. "It's not like Grantley High."

Her previous school, in Gloucestershire, had been

9

a girls' grammar, very staid and traditional. Most of the girls came from affluent homes, with parents who could afford to take them on skiing holidays and buy them horses – pocket money wasn't a problem. Ruth still hadn't recovered from the shock of her parents' decision to send her to the local comprehensive, now that they had moved down to Kent. Midway through the fifth year was far from being the ideal time to change schools, with GCSE course-work to consider, and it had been a question of finding her somewhere she could continue to take all her subjects and make use of all the course-work she'd already done. Someone Ruth's mother worked with had told her that the comprehensive always got very good exam results, and that had settled it. "After all, it's for less than a year," her mother had pointed out. "You can always change back to a grammar school for A-Levels."

Ruth still wasn't sure about the comprehensive. She wasn't sure whether she liked going to a school with boys in it; she was used to boys being kept in their proper places, strictly out of school hours, as boyfriends or other people's brothers, and some of the males in her form looked positively frightening: tall, confident and muscular. To her relief, however, they had so far paid her little attention, beyond staring curiously. In Ruth's first lesson, English, the only spare seat had been next to Melanie, who had smiled in a friendly manner and pushed her book over for Ruth to share. At the end of the lesson, though, the class had split up into separate Option groups, and

Melanie had gone off to Technical Drawing while Ruth had frowned at her timetable and tried to remember where the German room was. She thought Melanie looked more approachable than most of the other girls, and had been disappointed to find that they were only in the same group for registration and English.

The other waitress, an older woman, brought the champagne in an ice-bucket and poured a small quantity into Ruth's father's glass. Looking rather ill at ease, he sipped it and gave his verdict: "Very nice, thank you."

The waitress filled all three glasses. Ruth saw her mother's expression, a wry, amused smile. Ruth knew what that smile meant – it meant that these people, with their quaint provincial ways, didn't know how things should be done, as they were in the smart London restaurants she was used to frequenting for business lunches. There, used to high-powered businesswomen, the staff would have known that Ruth's mother should have been given the champagne to taste, as she had ordered the meal and she would be paying for it.

Ruth's father raised his glass and clinked it against his wife's. "Here's to your new partnership, Ginny – Morley and Webster. I wish you every success, darling."

"Thank you." Ruth's mother leaned towards him with a dazzling, intimate smile, so that Ruth suddenly wished she hadn't come; her parents would surely have

11

preferred to dine alone, without her tagging along. Her mother, as if reading her thoughts, glanced across the table at her and said, "And of course, to a rewarding year for Ruth."

Ruth wished she could feel the light-hearted gaiety usually associated with champagne. The problem with being an only child of such successful parents – her mother now a senior partner in a firm of solicitors and her father an illustrator of up-market children's books – was that it was taken for granted she would have a prestigious career herself. Her parents already had her future planned – A-Levels, university, then some upwardly-mobile and lucrative profession. Looking across the table at her parents, whose success seemed to cast a literal glow of radiance on them, Ruth thought that genetics worked in strange ways. She'd inherited her mother's looks and her father's small, fine-boned build, but why had neither of them passed on their confidence? She looked enviously at Melanie, who was crossing the restaurant with a tray of starters expertly balanced in one hand. Although Ruth had hardly spoken to her, Melanie somehow gave the impression of being quietly self-assured, of having inner reservoirs of strength and calm, qualities Ruth saw as thrown into relief by her parents' relentless ambition and drive.

Ruth sipped at her champagne, acknowledging her mother's toast, and wished that the phrase "a rewarding year for Ruth" didn't carry so obviously the unspoken meaning of "good exam results".

* * *

Returning to the kitchen with a trayload of used plates, Melanie scraped the leftovers, scraps of meat and bits of salad and half-eaten bread rolls, into the black-lined dustbin. She wasn't aware that Paul, the student helper, was watching her, until he remarked, "You'll never get used to it, will you?"

"Used to what?"

"The food going in the bin. All that waste." Paul was accustomed to Melanie exploding back into the kitchen after serving people with expensive food they didn't really want, over-fed businessmen worrying about their cholesterol levels or women wondering whether to abandon their calorie-controlled diets in favour of chocolate cream gâteau.

"I know I won't. It stares me in the face every night." Melanie could never stop herself from thinking that all the food served in the restaurant in one evening would probably feed an entire village in the Sudan for a week. She was naive, her father said. All restaurants wasted food, and so did all school canteens and transport cafés; it was inevitable, and couldn't make any difference to starving villages in Africa. Melanie stacked the plates in the dishwasher. It was naive, she knew, to think of the world's food supply as an enormous basket of bread which merely had to be shared out fairly – it was impractical idealism, yes, but surely such a simple and blazingly logical idea must have something to be said for it? All the arguments

13

politicians used, about technicalities like national debts and the EEC and grain mountains, obscured the real issues, the unfairness of wealthy people giving themselves weight problems and heart disease while others starved for want of a few grains.

"Anyway, I don't want to get used to it," Melanie concluded, banging shut the dishwasher door, "if getting used to it means I don't want to do anything about it."

Two

"Fund-raising? No thanks." Vicky rummaged in the back of her locker, dislodging a folder which was insecurely wedged on the top shelf, so that papers cascaded to the floor. "Damn. Now look what I've done. No, sorry, Melanie, you can count me out. I've got all this course-work to catch up on, or Miss Vine'll do me next week."

"Ask Balvinder," Lisa suggested, examining her reflection in a small pocket mirror and arranging a lock of hair to her satisfaction. "He's a Paki – he ought to help."

"Balvinder comes from Bengal, not Pakistan," Melanie told her coldly. "And I don't see the connection with famine in Africa."

"Same thing." Lisa looked at Vicky for appreciation of her wit, but found her friend engrossed in sorting out her spilled papers. "Anyway, as Vicky says, the rest of us just haven't got the time."

"Well, thanks a lot," Melanie said with heavy sarcasm. You could always rely on Lisa to say something utterly crass. Unfortunately, she was popular, and her response to the fund-raising appeal might influence others. Melanie looked round desperately for an enthusiastic face, and her eye lighted on Chris and Gary leaning against the wall, their heads, one fair, one dark, bent over a chess problem on a scrap of paper. "Gary, you're coming to the meeting, aren't you? And Chris?"

"Yeah, we'll be there," Chris said, looking up.

"Thanks. Well, that's a start, at any rate." Melanie couldn't resist giving Lisa a look of triumph.

At that moment the bell shrilled out its raucous note, signalling the end of break.

"See you later. And we'll bring Jon." Chris stuffed the newspaper cutting with the chess problem on it into his blazer pocket, shouldered his bag and set off along the crowded corridor.

The meeting was to be held at lunchtime in the form-room. Melanie, arriving early, rubbed a chalked message "VICKY WOZ ERE" off the blackboard and wrote impressively, "OXFAM FUND-RAISING COMMITTEE – INAUGURAL MEETING." She wondered how much response she could expect. All the teachers had been really laying it on thick recently about exam course-work and how little time there was left, and if even Vicky, one of the form's most notorious backsliders, was getting neurotic about work, it was a sure sign that all these warnings were having some effect. Having Chris and Gary involved was a definite bonus, though; both were popular, and might be able to wield some influence.

Her thoughts were interrupted by the arrival of Chris, Gary and Jon, a large boy with a pale, serious face.

"What's this all about then, Mel?" Chris asked. "Changing your surname to Geldof?"

"Or going for the Governors' special award for service?" Gary suggested.

"Not just me, I hope," Melanie said firmly. "I want everyone to be involved."

"*Everyone*," Chris repeated, looking round at the empty classroom. "Not much hope of that."

Melanie looked at her watch. "I said half-past. It's early yet."

"Here come some more now," Jon said, looking out into the corridor. "Matthew and Balvinder and that lot."

More people drifted in in twos and threes, sitting down on chairs and tables, and by the time Melanie started the meeting she felt she was addressing a reasonable-sized audience – so much so that her voice quavered slightly as she began to speak.

"I know we've all got a lot to think about this term, but I do think it's important for us to raise some money – a thousand pounds, I hope – for Oxfam. We're always hearing on the news about awful famines, and it's easy to take it for granted, to think nothing can be done about it. Well, maybe we can do something. I know a thousand pounds isn't much in terms of what needs to be done, but if we could raise that much we could perhaps buy a well for a village

17

in Africa. It's awful to just sit here and watch while people starve, while in this country we're all worried about being overweight." Melanie half-expected some joking remark at this point, as she was far from slim herself, though not through over-eating in her case. Nobody said anything, but out of the corner of her eye Melanie saw that her jibe had hit an unintended target; Jon, who was overweight to the extent that to call him plump would be a euphemism, gave an embarrassed wriggle. Melanie continued hastily, "So I hope you'll all want to join in."

"Yes, but join in what?" Chris asked after a pause.

"Well, I hoped people would organise things in twos and threes – raffles, cake sales, car washing – things like that."

"Don't we do enough on Comic Relief Day?" Matthew said.

"Comic Relief's great – we make a lot of money by wearing silly clothes and throwing water at each other, just for one day," Melanie said firmly, "but I want to do something that carries on after we put the red noses away for another year."

People began to mutter to each other, not looking very inspired, Melanie noted gloomily. After a moment Gary said, 'Well, I'm quite willing to raise some money, but wouldn't it be better if we all did one big, spectacular thing?"

"Like what?" Melanie asked.

"I don't know – a sponsored run, or something. You organise it, and we'll take part."

"I don't know about running," someone said. "I'd rather do a sponsored walk."

"We had a sponsored run last term to raise money for the minibus," Chris pointed out. "We need something different."

"Something unusual," Gary agreed.

"Perhaps the Committee should decide and let the rest of us know," said Balvinder, pointing at the blackboard. "Who's on the Committee?"

"Well, no-one at the moment," Melanie said. "Apart from me, that is. I thought that would be one of the things we could arrange today. Would anyone like to be on the Committee?"

There was more mumbling and then two hands were raised hesitantly. One belonged to Jon, and the other, Melanie noted with surprise, to Ruth, who was sitting by herself at the back of the group. Melanie had completely forgotten about her intention of asking Ruth to help with the fundraising.

"Jon and Ruth – thanks, you two. Anyone else?"

After a moment Chris said, "I don't mind."

"Good. That's four of us, then." Melanie wrote down the names, then said, "Well, suppose the Committee meets tomorrow, then reports back to the rest of the group? Can you all manage the same time on Friday?"

This was agreed, and Melanie summed up: "Right then, the Committee will try to think of some simple-to-organise, yet amazingly profitable and spectacular fund-raising venture, and we'll tell you what it is at the next meeting."

Jon hated PE. If it had been invented with the sole aim of making him embarrassed and uncomfortable, it could hardly have been more successful. For one thing, he was very conscious of his size and weight, and loathed having to appear in shorts and vest. Soccer wasn't so bad – he had monopolized the role of goalie, and could keep his tracksuit on – but gym lessons were bad news. Lumbering about the apparatus, trying to keep up some semblance of being purposefully occupied, Jon was acutely aware of his physical shortcomings. It was the only area of school life where Jon had to face failure – he was academically gifted to the extent that teachers were practically begging him to take their subjects at A or A/S Level. Jon got on well with all his teachers except Mr Evans, the head of PE; he and Mr Evans regarded each other with mutual contempt. Evans had a way of putting Jon down in an infuriating yet subtle manner. Nothing Jon could really complain about, but the patronizing tone in which he approved some minor feat – "Good *lad*, Shirley!" as if Jon were a podgy infant at his first day at playschool – made Jon grit his teeth in fury, feeling that he would have preferred a direct insult.

Jon saw with relief that the hands of the big gym clock pointed to three-fifteen. Time to put the apparatus away; P.E. was over for another week, and he could put his inadequacies away with his shorts and vest.

Mr Evans had other ideas, however. He appeared beside Jon, handing him a large bunch of keys. "Just nip along and give these to the caretaker, will you?"

"What, now? Can't I get changed first?"

"No time. I said I'd get them back to him by the end of school. He'll be waiting for them."

Jon wondered whether Mr Evans had planned this deliberately to humiliate him, knowing that the errand meant walking along the front of school to the caretaker's hut. It was bad enough having to appear in such scanty clothing in the gym, where Jon couldn't help comparing his own physique with Chris's and Gary's; they were as lean and athletic as Wimbledon tennis stars, making Jon feel like Winnie-the-Pooh as he stood beside them. But even this paled into insignificance beside the dreadful possibility of being exposed for all to see at the front of the building when the bell rang for the end of school. Jon hurried on his mission and thrust the keys into the caretaker's hand, calculating that even if the bell rang at that precise moment he would have time to get back to the gym before pupils began to emerge.

However, the caretaker said, "From Mr Evans, is it? Hang on a minute – I've got the screwdriver he was asking for," and Jon was forced to stand and wait while a lengthy search brought the correct screwdriver to light. By this time, the peace of the afternoon had been replaced by sounds of chairs plonking on desks and raised voices as children were released from their classrooms.

Jon set off, his heart sinking as he recognized a gang of rowdy fourth years among the pupils spilling from the main entrance. A joyous shout went up, "It's the Incredible Bulk!" which set off a gale of laughter, and further yells of "In training for the Olympics, Shirley?" and "What's it like to be a seventeen-stone weakling?"

Jon ignored them, but could feel the redness spreading over his face, which provoked more insults. He knew that Chris or Gary would have thought of some quick-witted response, turning the tables back on the taunters: "At least he's not a weedy little string-bean like you, Thompson," Chris had yelled back on one occasion. Jon wondered why, for all his brain-power, he simply didn't have the gift of witty repartee. He took it all too much to heart, he knew, storing each insult like a black mark against him. He kicked disconsolately at an empty crisp-packet.

At once a stern voice rang out from the deputy head's office. "Don't just kick it, boy! Pick it up and put it in the bin!"

The appropriately-named Mrs Paine was standing at her window, glaring at him as if he were a naughty first-year. God, did she have nothing better to do than stand there pouncing on minor misdemeanours? Jon snatched up the offending crisp-packet, stuffed it into the nearest litter bin and stomped off to the gym changing rooms. Most of the boys had gone now, only a few still cramming garments into their bags or tying their shoe-laces. Jon began to undress, feeling at an all-time low. A glimpse of himself in the wall-mirror as he removed his vest did little to cheer him up. He stopped changing and glowered at the reflection of his large, pale body. Melanie's remark at the meeting came back to him, about the immorality of people being overweight while others were starving. She made it sound as if he were personally responsible, carrying all that extra weight around on his body to represent food he shouldn't have had. Much as he liked Melanie, Jon felt bitter about that remark – after all, he'd taken the trouble to go along to her meeting, and had volunteered to be on her committee. She was no lightweight herself, being both tall and well-built, but for some reason people never teased her as they did Jon.

He padded off towards the showers. Nearly all the hot water had been used up, and a lukewarm trickle was the best he could produce. He soaped his despised body, wondering why he couldn't have been built like Chris or Gary. These two, being personable, friendly and good at games, were universally popular. Jon knew that he had more brains than either, but this only earned him the tag of "Boffin" to go with his other unwelcome nicknames. From the female point of view, Chris's blond, athletic good looks and Gary's dark curly hair and disarming grin clearly had far more appeal than Jon's consistent string of A-grades or prowess on the chessboard. Jon had, until recently, told himself that he wasn't particularly interested in girls yet, but was now beginning to think that perhaps he ought to be. His mirror image mocked him, reminding him again how slender his chances were of attracting any female who wasn't either desperate or chronically short-sighted.

He had made a few half-hearted attempts at losing weight, but his mother had always dissuaded him, saying that it was only puppy fat, and that he was a growing lad and needed lots of good food. But how long, Jon wondered, could he go on believing it was puppy fat? His mother would still be saying that when he was drawing his old-age pension. He couldn't go on putting it off any longer, he decided. It was definitely time to do something about it. He'd lose weight drastically, just to show Melanie and Mr Evans and those stupid fourth years.

He finished dressing, counted the money in his blazer pocket and set off homewards, making a slight detour in order to visit a small row of shops which faced the recreation ground. The newsagent's shop was empty of customers. Carefully ignoring the displays of sweets and chocolates, in spite of his rumbling stomach, Jon made for the magazines. Yes, there were several slimming magazines to choose from. They all seemed to be aimed at women, but Jon found one which seemed to meet his needs; it had a feature in it entitled "Do You Really Want to Lose Weight? Try our Quick and Easy Diet".

Leafing through the pages, he went up to the counter to pay, noticing too late that the middle-aged woman who had been at the till when he entered was no longer there. Instead, chewing gum and looking at his intended purchase with considerable interest, was Lisa from school, Chris's latest girlfriend. What Chris saw in her Jon couldn't imagine. She had obvious physical charms, but in Jon's eyes these entirely failed to compensate for her thoroughly unpleasant nature.

He felt himself turning scarlet. He half-turned away, then stopped, realizing it was too late to put the magazine back on the shelf. He would have to face up to it. He slapped the magazine defiantly down on the counter. "I didn't know you worked here."

"Started last week." Lisa shifted her chewing gum to the other cheek and gave him a malicious grin. "It's funny when you see what people come in and buy. You buying slimming magazines, for instance. I'd never have guessed you were into slimming."

"It's not for me. It's for my Mum," Jon lied. He counted out his money and placed it on the counter in a neat pile.

"Oh, yeah? Runs in the family, does it?" Lisa took the money, giving Jon a wide, insolent smile.

He turned and left the shop abruptly, cursing himself for not having walked the slightly further distance to Smith's in the High Street. He knew that Lisa hadn't believed his lie, and she would be certain to spread his secret to everyone she knew.

At home, the kitchen was filled with the warm smell of baking, and a large, solid fruit cake stood on a tray with teacups ready. Jon kissed his mother and threw his school-bag down in a corner.

"Had a good day, love?" Mrs Shirley asked, pouring out his tea.

"No, not really," Jon answered truthfully.

His mother's face clouded with concern. "Why, love? What happened?"

Jon hesitated. "Well, nothing much really, I suppose. I went to a meeting about Oxfam and we had P.E. And Mum – " he may as well tell her straight away, he decided – "I think it's about time I went on a diet. I'm fed up with being fat. And I've bought this magazine to find out all about it."

"Oh, but love." His mother was shepherding him into the front room, following him with the tea tray. "We've had all this before. I said then that you shouldn't worry about dieting while you've got your O-Levels."

"GCSEs, Mum, not O-Levels," Jon corrected automatically, sitting down on the sofa next to a large black-and-white cat.

"Well, anyway, there's plenty of time for that later. It's only puppy fat, I've said before."

"Yes, but how many puppies do you know as fat as I am – " Jon stopped, noticing his mother reaching for the cake-knife. "No cake for me, thanks, Mum."

"Oh, but it's your favourite. I only made it because you like it. Dad prefers a nice sponge."

She looked so disappointed that Jon was forced to give in. "Oh well, perhaps I will then. Thanks, Mum."

26

Chris and Gary both had mothers who went out to work, and they sometimes said that they envied Jon for having a homely mother who was always there to make him cups of tea and cook him big dinners. There were certainly advantages, Jon had to admit, in having a mother older than most people's, who had fixed ideas about women's roles and would hardly let him or his father lift a finger in the house. However, it was clear that dieting wasn't going to be easy.

Jon took a large bite of fruit cake. He'd have to start the diet tomorrow.

Three

Chris had had to wait so long to get into the bathroom that he was nearly bursting. When his mother emerged at last in her dressing gown, a heavily perfumed cloud wafted out with her.

Chris clutched at his throat theatrically. "Crikey, I'll need a gas mask to get in there. Are you going out?"

"Oh, just for a meal with a friend," Mrs Dunne replied.

Chris looked at her closely. "A friend" inevitably meant a male friend. Since his parents' divorce two years ago, his mother had had several boyfriends, none of them at all satisfactory from Chris's point of view. He wondered which it would be this time. The most recent in the series had been a good-looking estate agent who had seemed closer to Chris's age than his mother's.

"Anyone I know?" Chris asked.

His mother swept into her bedroom and sat down at her dressing table with her back towards Chris, indicating that she was not disposed to conversation.

"Oh, I shouldn't think so," she replied vaguely, opening a jar of skin cream. "Make sure Ian goes to bed at a reasonable time, won't you?"

"Yes, all right." Chris went into the bathroom and locked the door, feeling rather peeved. She hadn't even bothered to ask whether he was going out himself. He wasn't, as it happened, but he might have been, and who would have stayed in with Ian then? Besides, he felt uneasy about his mother's boyfriends, finding fault with all of them. He tried to push aside the idea that she might remarry, and someone new might try to take the place of his father.

When his mother eventually emerged from her room, fragrant and immaculate, he took in the details: her latest dress, high heels, dangling earrings, glossy lipstick – the whole works. It was only since the separation that Chris had realized his mother was still a young, attractive woman; she had bought new clothes and had her hair done differently, apparently needing to prove it to herself.

She kissed the air fractionally above his cheek, to avoid smudging her lipstick. "Bye then, love."

"Have a nice time. What time will you be in?"

"I don't know. Don't wait up for me."

Honestly, Chris thought when she had gone, you might think she was the teenager and he was the parent. He went into the lounge thinking vaguely of watching television, but Ian was sitting there engrossed in a cartoon. There was nothing he particularly wanted to watch, anyway. He considered doing some geography homework, but rejected the idea, deciding he wanted company. Lisa, he knew, would come round like a shot if he asked her to, but after a moment's consideration he phoned Gary instead.

"Are you doing anything this evening? Want to play some chess?"

"Nothing much. I'll come round, shall I?"

Half an hour later they were engrossed in silent contemplation of the chess pieces. Gary won the first game and Chris the second, surprising Gary with a sneaky move which robbed him of his queen at a crucial stage.

"Fancy an equalizer?" Gary suggested.

"Let's have some coffee first."

Chris dispatched Ian to bed, brought coffee and biscuits into the lounge, and put on a record.

"What d'you reckon Melanie will think up, for this Oxfam thing?" Gary remarked, sprawling back in an armchair.

"Dunno. She's bound to think of something. She always does."

"What do you think of that new girl?" Gary asked. "You know, that blonde girl, Ruth?"

Chris took a biscuit and munched it while he considered. "She's all right. Haven't really thought about it."

"A bit classy, I'd say."

"Definitely," Chris agreed. "Why, do you fancy her or something?"

"Yeah, I suppose so," Gary conceded. "Only she's a bit out of our class, isn't she?"

Chris lowered his coffee mug and looked at his friend critically. "I don't know about that. You can speak for yourself, but no-one's out of my class."

"Huh – modest. No, you might think no-one can resist you, but that Ruth isn't like the other girls we know. She comes from a snobby girls' school, for one thing. She talks posh. And have you seen the car her dad drives?"

"So what?"

"So, I reckon she doesn't like boys like us. She's probably already got some young stockbroker lined up. I bet not even you could get her to go out with you."

Chris couldn't resist a challenge like that. "I bet you I could," he said firmly. "But I thought you said you liked her yourself."

"Yes, but not seriously. I mean, I like lots of girls. I bet you wouldn't even get around to asking her out, though. Lisa would never speak to you again."

"That's up to her, isn't it? I can't spend my whole life doing what Lisa wants."

"Lots of people wouldn't mind."

Chris knew that many boys thought he was in an enviable position, going out with Lisa; she was extremely pretty, with pert features and considerable cheekiness. The trouble was, Chris thought, she knew she was gorgeous and expected everyone to admire her, as if it were her due. She was too confident by

31

half in his view, and for that reason he kept her at arm's length – metaphorically, not literally – so that she couldn't be too sure he'd always be available for her. He wanted to keep his options open, he supposed. He turned his attention to more pressing concerns, reaching for the box of chess pieces and placing them in position on the board.

"Let's play this equalizer then. You're black this time."

"A sponsored what?"

"A fast," Melanie repeated. "You know, going without food. Oxfam organize one every year, and people all over the country do it."

"I think it's a very good idea," Ruth said. "It's different, and easy to organize."

Chris hadn't taken much notice of Ruth before the conversation with Gary on the previous evening. Now he looked at her with new interest. He couldn't think why he hadn't been struck by her before. She was small and slim, with delicate features and a pale, clear skin, and although her hair was pale blonde her eyelashes were thick and dark, emphasising eyes as blue as his own. Perhaps it would be worth taking up the bet with Gary, Chris decided. However, that didn't necessarily mean falling in with Melanie's plans. Chris wasn't at all sure he liked the idea of going without food.

"But will people want to do it?" he asked. "I'm not

sure I do. I'm a growing boy – I need food. Can't we do a run instead?"

"Not everyone likes running," Melanie pointed out. "And Ruth's right, a fast is different. People will be more willing to give money for it."

"And it's got more to do with what we're raising the money for, hasn't it?" said Jon. "Going without food ourselves for a day, to raise money for people who haven't got food. I think we should do it."

"Well, obviously you wouldn't mind, Shirley," Chris said. "You're on a diet anyway. It might help you to lose an extra pound or two."

Jon gave an exasperated sigh. It had not taken long for Lisa to circulate the news of his diet around the form. "No, it's not that at all," he protested.

"How are we going to make sure people don't cheat?" Ruth asked. "When they go home after school, I mean?"

"I thought it might be best if we all stayed here at school for the night," Melanie explained. "Bring sleeping bags and stuff. It'd be more fun that way, and make it a bit out of the ordinary. But we'd need teachers to join in, because we wouldn't be allowed to do it unsupervised."

"But which of them would do it? Go without food and spend the night here?" Jon asked.

Several facetious suggestions were made before it was decided to approach Mr Scanlon, the form teacher. His subject was Humanities, but he also took part in various sporting activities, and was generally liked. "He'd do anything for a laugh," Jon commented.

However, when Melanie approached Mr Scanlon in his classroom at the end of school, his response was not encouraging. "You can go ahead and organize it if you like – with the Headmaster's permission, of course – but you'll have to ask someone else to supervise it for you. I couldn't go without food and do a full day's work, and anyway, I don't think it's healthy. We'd have people fainting all over the corridors. I'd join in if you were doing something different. I'm quite willing to raise money for Oxfam, but I'd rather not kill myself doing it."

"Well, there you are then," Chris said when Melanie reported her failure at registration next morning. "I told you it wasn't a very good idea."

"Of course it's a good idea," Melanie retorted. "You don't think we're going to give up at the first obstacle, do you?"

"Well, I thought the idea of a committee was that we should all agree what to do," Chris said, affronted. "You seem to have made your mind up already."

"What about Ms Vine?" Jon suggested, overhearing the conversation. "She's got an Oxfam sticker on her car. She might help."

Chris looked discouraging. "I think we ought to forget about the Fast, if Mr Scanlon didn't want to do it. He's keen on fitness and weight training and all that sort of thing, and if he says it's not healthy, perhaps he's right. He said he'd help out if we were doing something different, didn't he? That's what everyone else will say."

"Oh Chris, don't be such a wet," Melanie reproved. "I thought you'd come round to the idea."

"Well, we won't be able to do it anyway if none of the teachers will help," Chris retaliated.

However, Ms Vine, a youngish English teacher, was enthusiastic about the Fast, and agreed not only to help but also to try to co-opt other members of staff into taking part.

"So all we have to do now," Melanie told the other Committee members at their lunchtime meeting in the form-room, "is to get permission from the Head, and then – " she looked at Chris pointedly – "convince everyone else what fun it's going to be."

Chris decided that he didn't like being manipulated by Melanie. He had noticed that she always managed to get her own way without actually being bossy. He could imagine her turning out to be a headmistress or a politician or something when she was about fifty. She had completely ignored his opposition to the Fast, and was clearly going to go on with it no matter what he thought. "Well, you can do the Fast if you want," he told her. "I'd rather do something more positive. Fasting is only *not* doing something, isn't it? You do that, and I'll do something else with Gary and Mr Scanlon and whoever else is willing."

"There's no point in arguing among ourselves," Melanie said calmly.

Chris glared at her. "I'm not arguing. I'm just

expressing a different point of view. That's what committee meetings are for, isn't it?"

"Okay, Chris," Melanie said. "You want to do something exciting and physical and macho, is that right? What have you got in mind?"

"Anything you like," Chris said rashly. "And I bet we'll make more money than you will with your fast."

Melanie gave a triumphant smile. "You're on. Anything I like, you said? I'll think of something and let you know in a day or two."

"Here's his vaccination card," Mrs Shirley said, plonking it down on the kitchen table. "And don't forget to ask for the flea spray, will you, love?"

"Okay." Jon closed the lid of the cardboard pet carrier, receiving a disapproving glare from the occupant, a large, fat, black-and-white cat. He put the card into his pocket, heaved the box off the table, and manoeuvred his way through the narrow hallway and out of the front door.

The pet carrier was awkward to carry, swinging with the weight of the cat and bumping against his legs. By the time he'd reached the main road, he could feel the handle sagging, and wasn't at all sure it would last out the short journey. Monty, the cat, seemed equally critical. After a period of sullen silence, he gave a doleful yowl, and then began to scrabble fiercely at the floor of the box.

Jon put the box down on the pavement, resting his

aching arm. He crouched down and peered through the narrow slit in the side of the box which served as an air vent. "Look, pack it in, Monty," he told the disgruntled cat. "We'll be there in a minute. Anyway, you're always sick if we go in the car – you should be grateful."

As if by way of answer the cat swiped a paw at the air vent, claws distended and grasping firmly. Jon could see that the cardboard wouldn't stand up to this sort of treatment; it was starting to tear already. He'd have to hurry. He picked up the box again, this time clasping it to his chest instead of holding it by the handle, and set off at a fast walk.

The air vent was now at Jon's eye level, and through it he could see a large green eye. The next moment a paw appeared, tearing and clawing at the slit and widening it considerably, followed by the cat's head thrusting with determination through the enlarged hole.

"You stupid cat!" Jon felt like exploding with exasperation. He put the box down again to assess the situation. The cat had managed to push his entire head through the torn air vent, but was now firmly stuck, the edges of cardboard having closed around his neck. "Now look what you've done!"

Monty had the large head of a tom cat; it would be impossible for Jon to push his head back through the hole without hurting him. As far as he could see, the only solution was to tear open the side of the box, but how would he then manage the remaining distance

37

to the vet's? As Jon looked up to judge how much further it was, he saw a blonde girl coming towards him, carrying some kind of musical instrument in a black case: Ruth Webster. Why did fate have to conspire against him, Jon wondered, supplying a witness from school whenever he was in an embarrassing situation?

Ruth, however, came up to him looking concerned. "What have you got there?"

"My cat. I'm taking him to the vet's – it's not far, that red brick building along there – but he doesn't like being in his box, and now he's got himself stuck."

Ruth put her case down and bent to look at the cat. "Oh, isn't he *lovely*," she exclaimed.

Jon gave her a suspicious look. Fond as he was of Monty, he couldn't honestly have described him as lovely – he had a thuggish expression, one scarred ear, and a blodge across one eye which made him look like a lopsided panda. Nevertheless, Ruth seemed quite genuine in her admiration, stroking the cat's forehead and telling him he was a handsome boy.

"Well, he is quite nice," Jon conceded. "But I don't know what to do with him. I'll have to tear the box to get him out, and then I can't carry both him and the box."

Ruth stood up, pushing a lock of hair out of one eye. "I'll come with you. I live near here, in Manor Close, and I'm not in any hurry. Then you can carry the cat and I'll carry the box."

"Oh, would you?" Jon said with immense gratitude.

"That would make it much easier, if you really don't mind."

"No, honestly."

Jon freed the grumbling cat and they set off, Ruth carrying her violin case in one hand and the broken cat box in the other. She felt pleased of this chance to help Jon. It was hard changing schools in the fifth year, when friendship groups were already established; some people had merely ignored her, others had been openly hostile, and it was only rare individuals like Melanie and Jon who had actually been kind to her. Earlier in the term, as she had walked along the corridor one break-time, some girls she didn't even recognize had called out something in an exaggerated upperclass accent which Ruth supposed was intended for her hearing. Jon had caught her up and said rather shyly, "Don't take any notice of them. Some people in this school will make fun of anyone who's in the slightest bit different. I get fed up with it myself, I know what it's like.'

Ruth had been surprised, wondering what people found to tease Jon about. She had only gradually realized that it was because of his size, and thought it a pity that people kept on at him, it being so obvious that he was acutely sensitive. Even Chris, who was supposed to be Jon's friend, had made the odd hurtful remark in Ruth's hearing. Ruth knew that a lot of the girls admired Chris. She could see why they thought him attractive, with his rather sulky good looks and his dry sense of humour, but at the same time she found him rather awesome. Jon, on the other hand, was quite ordinary and reassuring. It would never have occurred to her to tease him about his size. He could just as easily have teased her for being skinny; what did it matter?

They reached the vet's and went into the waiting room, where Jon was relieved to see that the only other patient was a tabby cat in a wicker basket. There were no yapping dogs to upset Monty, who made no further attempts to escape, and looked around with interest.

"Have you got his vaccination card?" the receptionist asked when Jon had sat down.

"Yes." Jon shifted the cat on his lap to remove the card from his pocket.

"Here, let me take him," Ruth offered, sitting beside him.

Jon looked doubtfully at Ruth's expensive-looking pink lambswool sweater. "You'll get hairs on your jumper," he warned her.

"I don't mind," Ruth assured him, gathering Monty up and clasping him in her arms. Jon went to the receptionist's desk to confirm Monty's personal details.

At that moment a large Dobermann entered the waiting room, straining at its lead and pulling a small man after it. Monty stiffened in Ruth's arms, his green eyes staring. The Dobermann looked up, ears pricked alertly, and plunged forward, dragging its helpless owner across the waiting room. Monty gave a wail of fright; claws flailing wildly, he hauled himself out of

Ruth's grasp, shot across the room and cowered under a chair, hissing defiance.

Foreseeing a bid for escape through the open door, Jon sprang across the room and slammed it shut, startling the dog owner, who had ended up on his knees on the floor, still firmly grasping the leash. About to help him up, Jon stopped and stared at Ruth in horror. A long scratch ran down one pale cheek, beaded with tiny drops of blood. However, Ruth, taking no notice of her injury, dived under the chair, grabbed the cat and lifted him up, taking a firm hold of his collar.

"Oh Jon, I am sorry,' she gasped. "I just couldn't keep hold of him. It was a good thing he didn't get out of the door."

Jon was appalled. "Never mind that. Look what he's done to your face!" He raised a tentative hand. It would be dreadful if Ruth was scarred for life, all because of his incompetence.

Ruth touched her face and looked at the blood on her fingertips. "Oh, it's nothing – I hardly felt it."

The man with the Dobermann, the tabby cat's owner, and the receptionist clustered round to look, offering apologies, advice and sympathy. The vet, who had emerged from her surgery to see what the fuss was about, offered first aid, supplying cotton wool and a small basin. Jon took the cat from Ruth, his heart sinking further as he noticed a small brown stain on her pink sweater. "Oh God, look – he must have – "

Ruth looked down at herself. "You mean he – "

Jon didn't know what to say. "Sorry" sounded so inadequate. "He didn't mean to do it. It was the fright, you see, he always does that if he's frightened . . ." He faltered and stopped, aware that a discourse on his cat's bowel movements was hardly likely to improve the situation. A distinctive smell was already obvious. Christ, Ruth will never forgive me, Jon thought desperately. All because she'd been kind enough to offer to help. He knew he wasn't much good with girls, but Ruth had seemed so nice, and now what was the outcome of their meeting? Her face disfigured and her sweater covered in cat excrement. As an example of a classic boy-meets-girl situation it left a lot to be desired. She must wish she'd never set eyes on him or his cat.

"Ruth, I'm sorry," he began again. "Honestly, I don't know what to say – your face *and* your sweater . . . Will it wash out?"

"I expect so," Ruth said doubtfully.

When cleaned up, the scratch turned out to be a fairly shallow one, although to Jon's eyes the raised weal was horribly visible. The vet took Monty into surgery and administered the 'flu injection, and offered the use of a proper cat basket to ensure his safe return home.

"Look, Ruth, I'll walk home with you," Jon suggested as they left the surgery. "Manor Close is just round the corner, isn't it? You can't go home on your own like that."

"Honestly, I'm quite all right. You needn't worry."

"No, I want to," Jon insisted. "I feel responsible."

"Well, you needn't. It wasn't your fault at all."

Jon looked at her pleadingly. "Oh, *please*, Ruth. I shall feel awful if I just go home and leave you here with your face all scratched and your jumper ruined, after you tried to help me out."

"Oh, well, all right," Ruth said. "If you really want to. Thank you."

She looked at her watch anxiously. With luck, her mother wouldn't be home from work yet.

Four

Jon knew that Manor Close was a rather superior area, but even so he was surprised by the contrast between it and the nearby housing estates. A few detached houses – the sort estate agents described as "executive dwellings" – occupied the site of what had once been a manor in its own grounds; the area was still bordered by a sombre yew hedge, and a huge cedar cast sea-green shade over a smooth lawn in the centre of the close. Ruth seemed to be aiming for one of the larger houses, built in a traditional style of warm brick half-tiled in rusty red. Jon estimated that his own house would have fitted into a third of it.

A broad driveway swept up to a double garage with timbered doors. Ruth, her heart sinking as she saw her mother's Volvo parked outside, led the way towards an impressive porch.

"I'll leave Monty here in his basket, shall I?" Jon said as she unlocked the front door.

"Yes, okay, if he'll be all right there for a bit."

Ruth led the way through a wood-panelled entrance hall – Jon wiping his feet very carefully on the doormat before treading on the spotless jade carpet – and into an immense kitchen, where cream-coloured fitted cupboards and work-tops stretched away into the middle distance. A thin, dark-haired man, wearing a blue and white striped apron, was stirring something in a saucepan. He turned round with a welcoming smile as they entered, his gaze lighting on Jon with surprise.

"This is Jon," Ruth told him. "I've been helping him with his cat."

"Oh, yes," the man said vaguely. Then, looking at Ruth more closely, he noticed the scratch on her cheek. "Whatever's happened to your face, darling? Have you been in a fight?"

Jon stood hesitantly in the doorway. Was this Ruth's father, or some sort of cook? Just as he was deciding that a cook wouldn't be very likely to call Ruth "darling", quick footsteps could be heard descending the stairs. "Your mother's home early today," the man said. Jon thought he sounded apprehensive. He soon saw why. Ruth's mother strode in, high heels clicking, austere and officious in a dark grey pin-striped suit. She was youngish and quite attractive, with fair hair like Ruth's, but with none of Ruth's self-effacing manner. Her sharp grey eyes swept over Ruth and Jon as they stood against the fridge like stags at bay. She gave Jon a brief, formal smile, and looked to Ruth for an introduction.

"Oh . . . this is Jon," Ruth began. "He – "

"Hello, Jon." Ruth's mother barely glanced at him;

her attention was focused on Ruth's scratched face. "What have you done to your face?" she demanded.

Her tone of voice made Jon feel like a mugger who had attacked Ruth for a bit of fun. As mothers went, she was a completely different species from his own. The word "mother" to Jon conjured up a picture of a comfortably plump middle-aged person in a flowered apron. He couldn't imagine a less motherly-looking mother than Ruth's.

"It was a cat – Jon's cat," Ruth began to explain. "We were at the vet's . . . it was an accident . . ."

"Vet's? What were you doing at the vet's? I thought you were having your violin lesson."

Jon took over and launched into a detailed explanation, feeling himself withering under Mrs Webster's penetrating gaze. "I'm awfully sorry," he finished lamely. "And about Ruth's jumper, too."

Mrs Webster assessed the damage with a swift glance. "Well, really, Ruth. That sweater's almost new and it was quite expensive. You really could have been more careful. To say nothing of being scratched by a cat – you were lucky you weren't blinded. Is it vicious, this cat?" she added, turning to Jon.

"No, he was just frightened. He's in your porch in a basket, if you want to see him . . ."

"No, don't bring the animal in here, please – I'm allergic to cats. Has the scratch been seen to?"

"Yes, the vet bathed it for me and put something on it."

"It doesn't really sound as if it was anyone's fault,"

remarked Ruth's father, "and luckily the scratch isn't serious. It was good of Jon to come and explain."

"Yes. Thank you," said Mrs Webster coldly. "Now, if you can get changed and leave that sweater to soak, Ruth – *warm* water, not hot – supper's nearly ready."

"Er, yes, I'd better go," said Jon, taking the obvious hint.

Ruth went to the front door with him. She muttered, "Sorry about the third-degree. That's why I didn't want you to come round. But thanks anyway."

'I hope your face will be all right. I feel awful about it. And please let me buy you a new jumper, if the mark won't come out."

Ruth seemed embarrassed, as if she couldn't wait to get rid of him. "No, no, it really doesn't matter."

Carrying the cat basket out of the exclusive confines of Manor Close, Jon thought that he probably wouldn't be able to afford to replace the jumper anyway. If Ruth's mother had bought it, it had probably come from Jaeger or Harrods or somewhere equally unaffordable. He wondered what Ruth's parents would say to her now that he had gone. He felt sorry for Ruth, in spite of her plushy background, for having a mother like that. His own would have gushed concern and sympathy, not conducted an interrogation. It was surprising that Ruth was as nice as she was, he decided. Jon had an instinctive distrust of elegant and attractive girls, assuming that they would all be sharp and confident, like Lisa, and he had immediately put Ruth into that category. Now, however, he revised his opinion. A lot of girls would have made the most tremendous fuss over the cat incident, not taken it in their stride, as Ruth had. Imagine if it had been Lisa – Jon felt weak at the mere thought.

"Watcha, Shirley. What've you got there, a picnic hamper?" The voice behind Jon made him jump, and he turned to see Gary on his bike, decelerating to slow-bicycle-race speed to keep pace with Jon.

"It's Monty, my cat. I've just taken him to the vet."

Gary looked puzzled. "But your house is the other way from the vet's, isn't it?"

"Yes, well, it's a long story . . ." Jon hesitated briefly, then, casting caution aside, related the whole tale. To his dismay, Gary, instead of sympathizing, thought it was a great joke, swaying with laughter and making his bike swerve perilously. Anyway, Jon knew, everyone would be sure to hear about the farcical incident soon enough, when Ruth went to school next day with the scratch on her face clearly visible.

"You mean to say you got her covered in cat shit? God, Shirley, you really have a way with women, don't you? And you met Mummy and Daddy? I bet they were delighted."

"Well, it may sound funny to you, but it certainly wasn't at the time," Jon said with feeling. "Ruth was really nice about it, though. Imagine the fuss she could have made."

"She's all right, Ruth, isn't she?" Gary agreed. "Chris thinks so too. He's going to ask her out. I bet

48

him she wouldn't go out with him, being so upper class and all that."

Jon assimilated this piece of information, frowning thoughtfully. "Well, I don't think that's a very nice thing to do," he said finally. "Asking someone out for a bet. Suppose Ruth really likes him, and he's only doing it for fun?"

"Don't get your knickers in a twist about it," Gary said, back-pedalling. "He's not going to marry her, for God's sake. Don't take things so seriously."

Arrangements for the Sponsored Fast were going ahead. Melanie obtained permission from the Head, who had been most encouraging, congratulating Melanie on her initiative. The sponsor forms and an explanatory letter had been printed, and Ms Vine had got at least another six teachers to take part, although not all of them would remain in school overnight. Melanie's list of definite pupil participants now numbered more than twenty, and there were others who still had to get the go-ahead from their parents.

Melanie felt reasonably pleased with the response, although sometimes she found it hard not to show her impatience to objectors.

"Honestly, you should hear some of the excuses," she grumbled to Ruth. "'What's it got to do with us' – 'You don't know where the money will end up' – 'My dad says that it's their own fault' – " she mimicked.

"I know," Ruth sympathised. "Some people will believe anything rather than actually have to *do* something."

"Doesn't it occur to them," Melanie continued to fume, "that it's just their piece of luck that they were born in Kent rather than some Third World country? It's not asking much, is it, to go without food for just one day?"

As a direct result of reading Oxfam pamphlets and other literature, Melanie had decided to give up eating meat. This decision had been difficult to explain to her parents, who thought it was sheer perverseness.

"Most people would be *pleased* to have the choices you do, working in a restaurant," said her mother, who was writing out a list of the evening's special dishes in her beautiful calligraphic script.

Melanie tried to explain that it was partly because of working in a restaurant that she had become concerned about the wastage of food. "And meat is the most wasteful food of all. For every pound of steak, that animal has had to eat ten pounds of grain. And people are starving in the world for want of grain."

"Yes, but what about the grain mountains?" her mother had reasoned. "Why can't they be sent out to Africa?"

Melanie didn't pretend to understand the economics of agriculture, but she did feel it important to make some kind of change in her own life, even if it was only a token gesture.

"Anyway, you can't expect all our customers to become vegetarian overnight," her mother continued. "So you'll still have to serve meat, even if you won't eat it yourself. But I think it's cutting off your nose to spite your face. The animals are dead anyway, so what difference does it make whether you eat them or not?"

"It's the principle," Melanie insisted. "They wouldn't be dead if it wasn't for the fact that they've been bred for the meat market. They wouldn't have been alive in the first place."

Her mother drew a final flourish at the end of the desserts. "You'd have our customers eating a handful of plain rice and a crust of bread each, if you ran this place."

"It'd do them more good than steak and chocolate gâteau."

First thing on Friday morning, Melanie was collared in the driveway by Chris, who was still adamant in his refusal to take part in the Sponsored Fast, but wanted to know what alternative plans Melanie was making.

"I'm still working on it," Melanie told him. "I've got an idea, but it needs a bit of organizing."

"What have you got in mind?" Chris asked suspiciously. "Swimming the Channel? Walking from John O'Groats to Land's End? Crossing the Atlantic single-handed in a hot-air balloon?"

"You'll have to wait and see," was all Melanie would say.

Chris felt rather put out; he might as well have

organized a sponsored run after all, if Melanie still hadn't come up with anything better.

"I bet she's going to suggest something practically impossible," he grumbled to Gary, who had just arrived on his bike, "so that we have no chance of raising more money than her fast."

"Never mind that," said Gary, who was bursting with suppressed information. "You'll never guess what happened to Shirley last night . . ."

Chris enjoyed his Saturdays, working in his Dad's DIY shop. He and his father liked each other's company, and these Saturday meetings weren't spoiled by the rather fraught exchanges that took place at home on Sundays when his father called to collect his two sons for a day out. Chris hated to see his parents treating each other with frigid politeness, like strangers. "What time shall I expect them back?" "About seven-thirty, if that's convenient . . ." His father paid well, too, more than most people got for Saturday work.

Chris was kept busy, serving customers and bringing things in from the big shed at the back of the shop. During odd moments, he found himself thinking about the Sponsored Fast. Perversely, now that the idea had gathered momentum, he rather wished he were taking part. It would be a shame to miss it altogether, even though he wasn't going to give way to Melanie. Perhaps he and Gary could think of some way of putting in an appearance – they could say they were checking up that people weren't eating.

"Fancy going out for a bit of lunch, later on?" his dad suggested during a lull. "Bob won't mind. I can ask him to take his lunch break a bit early." Usually, one of them went out to buy rolls or sandwiches, which they ate in the untidy office.

On the way to the hamburger bar, Chris told his father about the Oxfam fund-raising, and the rivalry between himself and Melanie.

"Melanie's started all this off, has she? Good for her. I always liked Melanie. I'm sorry not to see her as much as I did when – " he checked himself – "as much as I used to." Chris had noticed that his Dad always tried to avoid any direct reference to his ex-wife. This caution was not shared by Chris's Mum, who had been known to refer to Jeff as "that bastard" in her sons' hearing. Chris hated that, feeling that he was being asked to take sides.

They sat opposite each other in the gaudy red-and-yellow plastic surroundings of the hamburger bar with loaded plates in front of them. Jeff was wearing a sweater Chris hadn't seen before, a traditional Fair Isle design knitted in many different shades of blue. He'd grown a beard recently; it was dark, like the rest of his hair, but Chris noticed grey hairs in it, the sight of them giving him a twinge of sadness. Jeff's hands holding his knife and fork were strong and brown, with flat, short fingernails – craftsman's hands.

"How's the woodcarving going?" Chris asked, pursuing this line of thought.

"Fine. I've just finished that walnut rocking-chair; it's turned out really well. Now I've got a beautiful piece of yew. I'm going to make it into a small table."

Chris had seen the rocking-chair in its early stages, and imagined his father working on it, conjuring the clean, sweeping lines of it, taking a sensuous pleasure in the beauty of the wood grain. He was always carving at something. It was one of the things that had so annoyed his wife, his habit of leaving slivers of wood lying about and appearing for meals with sawdust in his hair and eyebrows, and she had never liked the objects he made anyway, complaining that they took up too much space. Chris wouldn't let his mother sell the lovely old-fashioned painted rocking-horse his father had made for him when he was three; it was still upstairs in the loft.

"I might be getting myself a dog soon," his father said, spearing a chip. "Someone I know knows someone who's got a litter. A golden retriever."

"You always wanted one of those," Chris remembered.

"Yes. I can have it when it's ready to leave its mother, in a few weeks' time."

Jeff put down his knife and fork, looked at Chris as if about to say something else, then thought better of it and continued eating thoughtfully. Chris, eating steadily, noticed that his father kept giving him little apprehensive glances. He wondered what was up. He

54

was conscious of a faint glimmering of hope, which he tried to squash. It would be stupid to think that there was any hope of a reconciliation between his parents; he could see the differences between them only too clearly, but was still aware of a ridiculous wish that they might re-unite. He knew that his mother set great store by appearances, and his father was still undoubtedly a good-looking man, with thick, dark hair, and kind brown eyes beneath heavy brows. Could she forget all her grievances against him: his lack of ambition, his total absorption in his hobbies, his unsociable attitudes, his unwillingness to strive for bigger and better cars, houses and fridge-freezers?

"I was wondering whether you were doing anything in particular next Sunday," his father said at last. "If not, there's someone I'd like you to meet."

It was so at odds with what Chris had been thinking that it took him a few moments to take it in. "What do you mean, *someone*? Do you mean a . . . do you mean . . ."

"A woman, yes," his father said.

"Oh." Chris took a gulp of coffee, trying to re-organize his jolted feelings. His *father* had been seeing someone . . . he had got used to the idea of his mother having various male friends, but somehow this was more difficult to get used to, although he supposed no-one else would think it particularly surprising. He felt suddenly possessive about his father. "What's she like?"

"Well, her name's Lucy. You'll like her, I think.

She's quite a bit younger than me. She lives in London, but she's coming down to stay, next weekend. I thought we could all go out for the day – Lucy, me, you and Ian."

Chris said nothing, still trying to adjust. Of course, his idea of his parents getting together again was ludicrous; why had he ever contemplated it? The gulf between them had widened rather than narrowed. You only had to look at the outward signs – his mother, with her permed hair and trendy clothes and new boyfriends, trying to shed fifteen years, and his father with his beard and Fair Isle sweater (had this Lucy knitted it for him?) and the retriever puppy he was going to get. The really amazing thing was that they'd ever been attracted to each other in the first place.

"Don't look so aghast," Jeff said, rather embarrassed. "I'm only thirty-nine – I'm not completely over the hill yet. Your mum has lots of boyfriends, from what I gather."

"Yes, I know. It isn't that – it's just that I . . . Oh, I don't know what I mean . . ." Chris lapsed into silence, while his father looked at him in concern.

"I'm sure you'll like Lucy. She's good fun, very easy to get on with. You will come, Chris, won't you?"

Five

Melanie, on her way to English, stopped to wait for Ruth by the lockers. "What's all this about you and Jon and a cat?" she remarked.

Ruth pulled a folder out of her locker with a savage tug. "I just saw him on the way to the vet's, that's all, with his cat box all broken. I don't know why he had to tell the entire school about it."

Melanie examined Ruth more closely. "I must say, the scratch on your face doesn't live up to the rumours. I was expecting a great long bloody gash with stitches in it."

"Sorry to disappoint. But honestly, Melanie, it was such a silly little thing and yet I've heard about nothing else all morning. Don't people have anything else to do apart from gossip?"

"A lot of them, no. But Jon's not like that."

Ruth would have agreed with Melanie on this point until today. Now she felt that she couldn't forgive Jon for making the whole thing into a joke, and broadcasting it to everyone he saw.

"Cheer up," Melanie said, noticing Ruth's downcast

expression as they made their way towards the English classroom. 'It'll all be forgotten by tomorrow."

"Not by me, it won't."

When they got to the English room, Ruth got her books out and began turning the pages of her folder as a way of avoiding looking at Jon, who came in and sat down at the back of the room. Behind him, Lisa trailed in scuffing her feet, dumped her bag on the desk behind Ruth's, and sat down heavily beside Chris.

"Poems again. What on earth do we have to do poetry for?" she asked him sulkily. "When we go for job interviews, they're not going to ask us to stand there and recite stupid poems, are they?"

Chris opened a battered folder and took out a page of scruffy notes. "We've got to do some of everything, poems, stories and plays. Otherwise we can't enter for Literature."

"Well, it's bloody boring." Lisa delved in her bag, produced an opened bag of crisps and passed them to Chris. "Want some? I don't know about you, but I need something to help me get through the next hour. The only good thing about doing poems is you don't have so much to read as when we did that awful boring story."

Melanie turned round in exasperation. "Honestly, Lisa, you are a Philistine," she remarked. "*All Quiet on the Western Front* was a fantastic book, not hard to read at all."

"Who asked you?" Lisa retorted through a

mouthful of crisps. "And anyway, it was a boys' story. Why should we be interested in war and death and all that?"

Before Melanie could answer, Ms Vine strode into the room. As usual, she carried a smart black suede briefcase which contrasted oddly with her otherwise rather hippyish appearance: long wavy hair, navy woollen tights and brown leather sandals, several layers of droopy garments, and strings of ethnic beads. She plonked the briefcase on her desk, noted the crisps at once and told Lisa briskly, "Late breakfast or early lunch, it'll have to wait." She got a pile of paperback books off the shelf and told the two people nearest her to hand them out.

"*Selected Poems of Thomas Hardy* – well, this looks really exciting," Lisa muttered to Chris, before she was silenced by a glare from Ms Vine. Ms Vine might look like a remnant from the era of love-and-peace, but nobody played up in her lessons.

Chris didn't entirely share Lisa's aversion to poetry – the ones they had read about the First World War had been gripping stuff – but nevertheless the book in front of him didn't look too appealing. Ms Vine began talking about Thomas Hardy's novels, and why he had changed to writing poetry instead. Usually, Chris liked Ms Vine's lessons; she had a way of making the most difficult ideas understandable and relevant. Today, though, he found his attention wandering, his thoughts drifting towards the weekend ahead and the outing with his dad's girlfriend. Ian had greeted the idea with excitement, but Chris wasn't so sure. What would it be like, trying to make conversation with someone who had designs on his father? Would she really be interested in the two boys, or would she merely feign interest to make a good impression? When Chris had told his mother about the proposed outing, she had greeted the news with tight-lipped disapproval; Chris knew that he would face a grilling about the girlfriend as soon as he got in . . .

"Are you with us, Chris?"

Ms Vine's sharp voice jerked him back to the present; he looked across at Lisa's book for the page number, and leafed through his book hurriedly. Ms Vine, in a completely changed tone, began to read. Chris had missed her introductory remarks; the poem looked really simple, nothing to it at all, about frozen plants in a greenhouse. Wondering what on earth he would be able to say about it if he had to write an essay, Chris paid closer attention to the next one. It was about Thomas Hardy watching another man who seemed to be digging for relics on a Roman grave-mound, but who on inspection turned out to be burying a dead cat. The images of the fluffy white cat, lying dead in its basket, and the lonely man digging a little grave for it, concerned not for the past splendours of Rome but for the loss of his pet, produced a sudden and quite unexpected prickling at the back of Chris's eyes and an odd feeling in his chest. To his alarm, his eyes actually began to water; he blinked rapidly, aware of Lisa beside him and what she would think of him

– Christ, he was practically *crying* over a dead cat in a poem. What on earth was the matter with him? He didn't even like cats. It was a quite inexplicable feeling, and one which seemed to have by-passed his brain and gone straight for his tear ducts. He rubbed at his eyes furtively, hoping Lisa wouldn't notice. If she did, he had no doubt that it would soon be all round the fifth year – Chris, the hard man, the macho sportsman, crying over a Thomas Hardy poem . . . it didn't bear thinking about.

Fortunately, Ms Vine didn't notice, but went straight on to talk about the death of Hardy's wife and the poems he had written immediately afterwards. Chris wondered why he was able to listen to these with no outbreaks of excessive emotion, while the death of a cat had almost reduced him to tears. There was no logic to it, he told himself. His hormones must be unbalanced, or he was going down with 'flu, or something.

By the end of the lesson, Chris, feeling more normal but anxious to evade Lisa's clutches, darted out of the room as soon as Ms Vine dismissed the class. A good kick-about at football would make him feel better, he decided, looking for Gary, who was in a different set for English.

"If you've got a minute, Melanie, we could make sure everything's arranged for the Fast on Thursday," Ms Vine said, putting her books into her briefcase. "And Ruth and Jon, you're involved too, aren't you?"

Ruth hesitated, seeing Jon geting up from his seat.

61

"Sorry, I can't stay at the moment. I've got to see Mrs Craddock about something."

"Oh well, Melanie will no doubt put you in the picture later," Ms Vine said. "Right, we've got official permission now from the Town Hall, and the Head wants you to contact the local press, Melanie. They'll probably send a photographer round and do a short feature. How's the sponsorship going?"

"Fine. I should get about twenty pounds myself, and quite a few people are getting more than that."

"That sounds promising. Now, what about sleeping bags and blankets and all that sort of thing . . . ?"

By the time Melanie and Jon reached the dining hall, most of their year had been and gone. Melanie collected her meal from the serving hatch while Jon, who had brought a packed lunch, went straight to a table and sat down. Joining him, Melanie noticed that his lunch box contained crispbread, carrot and nut salad in a carton, and two sticks of celery.

"Oh, you're dieting, aren't you? How's it going?"

Melanie was one of the few people Jon didn't mind mentioning his diet.

"It's okay. I've already lost a little bit of weight. They tell you not to weigh yourself every day, but I can't resist. It's hard work though." He reached into his bag and produced two pages cut from a slimming magazine. "Look at this menu. For lunch you're supposed to have things like three ounces of cooked potato, or a salad made with two ounces of avocado and half an ounce of almonds and two black olives and two teaspoonfuls of dressing. You have to get up half an hour earlier to cut it all up and weigh it. And you're not allowed any snacks – what they call a snack is one small cup of coffee with skimmed milk. It's difficult when I'm used to my mum's home-made steak and kidney pudding and fruit cake. And Mum and Dad are putting back all that stodge every night, while I chomp my way through an enormous salad. Mum thinks I'm mad."

"Well, I think you're doing well to stick to it. I suppose I should lose weight myself," Melanie said ruefully, grasping a handful of her well-covered waistline, "but I never really think about it much. I'm just well-built, and I'm obviously going to stay that way. At least," she added, "on Thursday you won't have to worry about getting up early to make your lunch, because you won't be having any."

"That's a big consolation," Jon said drily. "How much money do you reckon we'll make from the Fast?"

"So far it adds up to about three hundred pounds. It's a long way short of the thousand I was hoping for."

"But what about Chris and Mr Scanlon and Gary? They say they're going to raise more money than you do. If they're going to beat your three hundred pounds, it'll have to be something pretty spectacular."

"Yes," Melanie agreed. "That's what I've got in mind."

* * *

Early on Thursday morning Melanie sat in the restaurant kitchen eating muesli, concentrating hard.

"You don't look as if you're enjoying that, love," her mother commented, noticing Melanie's intent expression.

"I am enjoying it. It's my last food for twenty-four hours. I'm making the most of every mouthful."

She left for school early, to meet the other fasters in the form-room. Their sleeping bags and other personal belongings were to be taken to the sixth form common room, where they were to spend the night. The participants also brought with them a packed breakfast for the following morning; this was to be taken away and locked in a cupboard, so that no-one could cheat.

"I'm hungry already," Balvinder complained, handing over a Tupperware container.

"Well, you'd better get used to it then."

"We've got to write an essay under exam conditions in History this afternoon," said Balvinder's friend Gregory. "All you'll be able to hear will be our stomachs rumbling. Luckily Mr Benson's fasting too, so he'll be just as bad."

Lunchtime was the worst point in the day, Melanie found; although she knew she wouldn't be having anything, thoughts of food kept rising to the surface of her mind.

"Are we really not even allowed a hot drink?" someone asked her.

"Yes, as long as it's only hot water," Melanie replied firmly.

Immediately after school, everyone gathered hungrily in the common room.

"It's going to seem a very long evening," Ms Vine remarked, "without all the usual cooking and eating and washing-up and cups of coffee. I suppose you've thought of that?" she asked Melanie.

"Yes. Most of us have got homework to do, then Balvinder's brought in a video film to watch later, and Mr Benson said he was bringing Trivial Pursuit."

"Good. Well, I'd better get on with some marking. Is the water urn here? I'm dying for a cup of hot water!"

"We may as well go and fetch it now, Ruth," Melanie suggested, "so that it's here ready to make tea and coffee in the morning."

"Okay. Where is it? In the Staff Room?"

As they returned along the corridor, hauling the urn along on its trolley, they were met by the Headmaster and two strangers: a woman with a notebook and a man with a camera.

"Ah, here's Melanie," the Head said as she approached. "The master-brain behind all this."

"Anne Furlong and Geoffrey Simmonds, from the *Chronicle*," said the young woman. "We'd like to take some photos of everyone taking part, and then ask you a few questions, if you don't mind."

The Headmaster led the way to the common room, and various ideas were discussed for a photograph which would convey the idea of people not eating. Various poses were suggested and tried, until finally the photographer hit on the idea of everyone sitting on the floor with empty plates in front of them. Plates were fetched from the kitchen and several shots taken.

"Now, Melanie, perhaps you can give me the details. What made you want to organise the Fast?" Anne Furlong asked.

Melanie felt very self-conscious, answering the questions and watching Anne Furlong carefully write down her answers, while the Headmaster looked on approvingly. He knew a good public relations exercise when he saw one, Melanie thought; he hadn't said anything about joining in, and she supposed he'd be going home soon and having a meal.

When the short interview was over, she went round to the main entrance with the Head and the two visitors. It was already almost dark; the silhouettes of the mobile classrooms and the caretaker's hut were black against a grey cloud-streaked sky. It felt strange saying goodnight to the Headmaster as he stepped through the main doors, and watching the caretaker lock up from the outside. She ran through everything in her mind, hoping she hadn't forgotten some important detail. She'd bought the milk and the tea and coffee for breakfast; she had a supply of glucose tablets in case anyone was in danger of fainting with hunger; she'd read up about the symptoms of hypoglycaemia. She felt very glad that Ms Vine and Mr Benson were staying in school with them, and would take charge if

66

anything awful did happen. She couldn't help feeling a surge of pride at the thought of all those people, raising money at her suggestion; but she tried to suppress the pride, reminding herself that it was only due to her good fortune that she was in a position to raise money for food aid, rather than being one of the people in Africa in such dreadful need of it. She no longer felt hungry, but as she walked along the gloomy corridor, her legs felt odd, as if they were walking by themselves, not quite attached to her body.

"Everything all right, Melanie?" Ms Vine greeted her.

"Yes, thanks. They took down all the details and said it'll be in next week's paper."

The common room looked quite cosy now; the curtains were drawn, and several people had spread out their sleeping bags and pillows to lie on while they watched TV. An intense game of Trivial Pursuit was taking place in one corner of the room. Jon and Balvinder were playing chess, and Jon, who was usually considered unbeatable, was losing. He had already surrendered a rook and a bishop to Balvinder, having quite failed to spot some fairly obvious strategies. Balvinder was crouched over the board with suppressed excitement, hardly able to believe he was winning, while Jon's glance kept straying across to Ruth, who was joining in the Trivial Pursuit.

Suddenly the peaceful atmosphere was interrupted by a loud banging on the window from outside, and shouts of "Let us in!"

"Who on earth's that?" Ms Vine asked. "None of you have invited any friends round, I hope? The Head said only those taking part were to stay here."

Balvinder, kneeling on a chair, pulled the curtains aside. "It's only Chris and Gary. We might have guessed they wouldn't be able to stay away."

Melanie crossed to the window and looked out at the grinning faces. "You can't come in," she told them. "Everything's locked up."

"Open the window and we'll get in that way," Gary shouted. "We only want to come in a for a little while."

Ms Vine nodded assent, and Melanie unfastened the window and swung it upwards. A denim-clad leg appeared, swiftly followed by the rest of Gary, and then by Chris, tumbling down over the arm-chairs and pulling a carrier-bag after him.

"Just wanted to see how you were getting on," Gary explained, with, Melanie thought, a suspiciously innocent smile.

"Oh, yes?"

"You don't mind if we eat our tea, do you?" Gary took a red box out of the carrier bag, and lifted the lid to reveal two plump, steaming hamburgers. He handed one to Chris and took a huge bite out of the other.

This gesture was greeted by shouts of outrage from all corners of the room.

"Get out!"

"Give us a bit!"

"Ooh, is that food? I've forgotten what it looks like."

"Take it away, for God's sake – the *smell* – you can't do this to us . . ."

Chris gave Melanie a sheepish smile. "Just testing your determination."

"We're determined all right. But if that's all you can contribute towards the Fast I think it's pretty pathetic," Melanie snapped.

"Oh, come on, Melanie," said Gary, his mouth full of hamburger. "It's only meant to be a joke."

"Well, it's not a very funny one," Melanie retorted. However, looking around, she became aware that most people did think it funny. Changing her tone, she said with heavy sarcasm, "It was nice of you two to drop in. Can we offer you a mug of hot water?"

"No thanks, we've brought our own liquid refreshment." Gary upended the carrier bag and tipped out two cans of Coke. "We want to stay and watch the film, if you don't mind, Melanie – grovel, grovel."

Melanie appealed to Ms Vine. "What do you think?"

"Well, as long as they go immediately afterwards, and if they're prepared to take the risk of being lynched by the starving mob."

"All right then. But eat those revolting hamburgers *quickly*."

Gary sat down on one of the armchairs. Opening his can of Coke, he looked around the room with interest. "Watcha, Shirley," he called across to Jon.

69

"How's it going? It's easy for you, I suppose – you can live off your reserves."

Jon flushed with annoyance. It was bad enough being teased, but the fact that Ruth was listening made it worse.

"It's the same for me, then," Melanie pointed out. "But what you don't seem to appreciate, Gary, is that we're better designed for survival than you are. We're far more efficient converters of food energy. You've got a higher metabolic rate, so you burn it all up quicker and need more. If we were ever short of food, I'd survive far better than you would."

"Blimey, are you taking A-Level Science or something?" Gary mumbled.

"No, it's just common sense."

Jon gave Melanie a look of admiration. Why hadn't he thought of saying something like that? Not only had she diverted attention away from his embarrassment; she'd also achieved the rare feat of silencing Gary, who finished his hamburger without another remark.

When the Trivial Pursuit game was over, Ruth clambered across the chairs and sleeping bags, got out her Maths homework and took it to one of the tables at the back of the room. Chris watched her. Thinking of his bet with Gary, he followed her over.

"Hey Ruth, do you know how to do those simultaneous equations?"

"Yes."

"Could you just do one or two with me? I didn't

quite get the hang of it in the lesson."

"Oh, all right." Ruth gave him a surprised look. She had thought that Chris was good at maths; he was always answering questions correctly in lessons. And why hadn't he asked Jon, who everyone knew was brilliant at Maths? She solved the first equation quickly, writing down the workings-out in her small, neat writing. Chris sat close beside her, looking at her dark lashes and her slender eyebrows drawn together in a frown of concentration.

"There." Finishing the equation, she glanced up and saw that Chris wasn't looking at her Maths book at all. His eyes, as blue as a Siamese cat's, met hers.

"Sorry, you're too quick for me. Can you do another one, going through all the stages?"

Across the room, Jon looked unhappily at their two fair heads close together. He must have been stupid to think that there was any chance of Ruth liking him. Chris, with his easy manner, good looks and popularity, would be a far better match for Ruth, his charm contrasting favourably with Jon's own ham-handedness. Chris would win his bet, Jon was certain. He could only hope that Chris would genuinely like Ruth, and not take advantage of her good nature.

"Come on, Balvinder, where's this video?" Ms Vine asked when the TV programme was over.

"In my bag. Shall I get it now?"

The film Balvinder had recorded, *State of Emergency*, was to be the main entertainment of the evening. Balvinder wheeled out the TV into a central position, and everyone crowded into a semi-circle round it, reclining on armchairs or sleeping bags and pillows.

The blurred lines on the screen resolved themselves into a large close-up of a succulent doughnut, oozing cream and jam, while an equally succulent voice-over drawled in praise of fresh cream cakes. The next advertisement was for farmhouse soup, with shots of a steaming bowlful and a hunk of crusty bread.

"You could have edited out the adverts, Bal!" a voice said indignantly. "This isn't fair to our stomachs!"

Wails of distress greeted the next advert, which was for gravy, and showed platefuls of roast dinner with someone pouring a shining stream of gravy over golden-brown roast potatoes, mounds of cauliflower and thick slices of rich brown beef.

"Did you do this on purpose, Bal?" Gregory demanded.

Balvinder sat looking puzzled as yet another food advertisement followed, this time for strawberry dessert. "I'm sure I played the beginning of the tape this morning, to check I had the right one. It started with the end of the nine o'clock news."

"You mean this isn't the film at all?"

"What's this one, then?"

Melanie noticed that Gary was wearing his nonchalantly innocent look, while Chris was keeping himself well hidden at the back of the group.

"Pehaps Gary and Chris have something to do with it?" she suggested.

72

Gary's eyebrows shot up in simulated astonishment. "Me?"

"Obviously, yes," Ms Vine said drily. "Come on, Gary, you may as well confess."

Gary's expression of indignation gave way to a broad grin. "Well, it was Chris who thought of it – "

"But Gary who insisted we actually did it – " Chris added.

" – and we had to spend ages sitting by the TV waiting for the right kinds of advert. I hope you appreciate the effort we've put in on your behalf – " Gary was silenced by a flood of abuse and by a flying pillow which caught him full in the face.

"Really, you two are incorrigible," Ms Vine said amiably. "And when did you change the tapes over?"

"Lunchtime, when Bal left his bag in the form-room. We hoped he wouldn't notice it was a different kind of tape. Here's the real one, in this bag."

Hunger was beginning to make Melanie feel light-headed. "Just you wait till tomorrow," she said. "I've got a little surprise for you two. I can wait that long to get my own back."

Six

Gary poked his head round the common room door
and raised his eyebrows at the sight of people sitting
on the floor eating breakfast.

"You're all still alive, then?"

Balvinder, eating cereal, remarked, "You sound
disappointed. Were you two hoping to help carry out
the corpses?"

"Well, yes. This is a bit too dull."

Chris followed Gary into the room. "Have you
counted everyone this morning, Melanie? Shouldn't
you make sure there isn't someone curled up dead in
a sleeping bag?"

"We're all fine, thank you," Melanie retorted, filling
mugs with hot water from the urn. "Nothing to it at
all. I can't think why you didn't join in. Now if you
want to do something useful instead of making silly
jokes, you can hand round these mugs of tea. There's
only fifteen minutes till registration."

"All right," Chris said grudgingly. "But only if you
tell us what this secret plan is you've been concocting."

"Oh, yes." Melanie handed him a tray of tea. "You

74

said you wanted something physical and macho, didn't you? Well, I think what I've arranged for you should fit the bill."

"Come on then, what is it?" Gary demanded.

Melanie said calmly, "A parachute jump."

Tea sloshed out of mugs and flooded the tray before Chris could steady himself.

"Good joke, Melanie, ha ha," he said, recovering slightly. "Hunger must have gone to your head."

Gary clapped a hand to his chest in a melodramatic attitude of shock. "Honestly, Melanie, you shouldn't tell me things like that first thing in the morning," he complained. "You *are* joking, aren't you?"

"Of course not." Melanie looked at the two boys with amusement. "It's all arranged. You'll train all day and jump in the evening. In two weeks' time. And," she added triumphantly, "Mr Scanlon thinks it's a great idea. He's looking forward to it."

Gary flopped down on a floor cushion. "You're mad. You're definitely mad. You seriously expect us to jump out of a plane?"

"That's right. You wanted something spectacular, didn't you?"

"Have you really made all the arrangements, Melanie?" Ms Vine asked.

"Yes. It's with a parachute club near Oxford. Someone Mr Scanlon knows learned to jump there, and he said the instructors are really good. Mr Scanlon will provide the transport. All that's needed is parents' permission. Everything else is all arranged."

75

"I bet she she's made arrangements for your funerals, as well," Balvinder said. "A sponsored burial. Here, give me that tray, or we'll never get any tea."

Chris and Gary were both looking slightly pale. Chris had realized his mistake in asking Melanie to reveal her plan in the presence of all these witnesses. Everyone knew about the challenge now, and everyone would know if he and Gary chickened out.

"Are you sure that's all you want us to do, Melanie?" he asked sarcastically, playing for time. "You wouldn't prefer us to climb the north face of the Eiger, or swim over Niagara Falls for you? You only have to say."

"Are you really going to do it?" Gregory asked admiringly.

"Crikey, I wouldn't," Balvinder said with emphasis. "Did you read in the papers about that bloke who . . ."

"It's all perfectly safe, with trained instructors to tell you what to do," Melanie cut in swiftly. "You don't even have to pull your own ripcord. It's done automatically."

"God, I'm scared of going up in planes, let alone jumping out of them," Gary muttered to Chris. "What do you reckon?"

Chris's eyes roamed around the room, his thoughts racing. His eye fell on Ruth, who was gazing at him in a rather awe-stricken way, and it occurred to him that doing the jump might be a way to boost his esteem

76

with her, as well as with the rest of the school's female population. On the other hand . . .

"It seems to me, Melanie," he said crushingly, "that it's very easy for you to stand there wittering on about how safe it is, when it's not you that's got to do it. There's a big difference between just fasting for a day, and leaping out of a plane at God knows how many feet, don't you think?"

Melanie paused to make sure everyone heard her answer. "Yes, there is a big difference. That's why I've booked four places on the course. You don't think you're going to have all the fun, do you? I'm going to do the parachute jump myself."

"She must be mad. She must be stark raving loony," Gary repeated for the twentieth time that day as he and Chris collected their bikes from the racks. "Can you think of any other girl who'd even think of something like that, let alone want to do it herself?"

"No." Chris hoisted his bag over his shoulders and mounted his bike thoughtfully. "Still, she's given us a bit of a poser, hasn't she? Either we've got to leap out of her damned plane with her, or she'll do it without us and we'll look like wimps."

"Do you really think she's got the guts to do it?"

"Yes," Chris replied without hesitation. Melanie had more determination than anyone else he knew. "The question is, Gary my old son, whether *we've* got the guts to do it."

"Why on earth didn't we do her sponsored fast?" Gary moaned. "It'd all be over by now, and it'd have been so easy."

They cycled down the school drive, weaving through straggling pupils, and out on to the road. Chris imagined himself edging out of a plane, taking that enormous irrevocable step forwards (or was it backwards?), plummeting through the sky . . .

"There is one thing," Gary suggested, drawing alongside Chris. "Our parents might not give us permission."

"True. But if they don't, and Melanie goes ahead, that won't help us much. We're going to look pretty feeble, aren't we, standing there saying, 'Well, we would have done it, only our mummies wouldn't let us.' That'll really impress everyone."

"I'm going to tell my mum all about how dangerous it is."

"No, it's no good. We're going to have to do it. You never know," Chris added with an attempt at optimism, "it might be fun."

"*Fun*. Yeah, I bet it's great fun to be scraped up on to a stretcher and spend the rest of your life flat on your back in hospital."

"Oh, shut up," Chris said amicably. They had reached Gary's turning. "I'll phone you tomorrow, and we'll decide what to do. Don't spoil your weekend worrying about it."

"I'll have nightmares," Gary called over his shoulder as he turned the corner into his road. "I'll be dreaming about parachutes that don't open, and crash landings and power cables and broken legs and ambulances . . ."

His voice trailed off into the distance, and Chris pedalled on alone, thinking about the dilemma he was in. Melanie had really manoeuvred him into a corner, and staged it so that the entire fifth year would know about the challenge she'd issued. She certainly knew how to get her own way. Chris was aware of a grudging admiration for her. You had to hand it to old Melanie, she'd really got the better of him so far. Chris found himself grinning irrepressibly as he cycled along the quiet suburban streets. He hoped his mother would be in a good mood tonight, and would agree to give him permission to do the jump. He'd already made up his mind that he wasn't going to be outdone by Melanie. He began rehearsing phrases in his mind, to present the idea of a parachute jump in as innocuous a light as possible.

"Do I really have to stay in?" Ruth asked disconsolately, hovering in the dining room.

Her mother placed a tall vase of lipstick-red tulips in the middle of the table and stood back to look critically at the arrangement. "Yes, of course. Where else can you go? And anyway, I've invited Marcus to be company for you."

"I don't want company. Couldn't I go round to Melanie's?"

"The girl whose parents own the restaurant? But she'll be working, surely, on a Saturday night," Mrs Webster pointed out, tweaking a wayward tulip into position.

"I could help her."

Mrs Webster ran a hand over the silky surface of the black ash table. "Oh, do stop complaining, Ruth, and don't be so ridiculous."

"I bet Marcus is horrible," Ruth grumbled, "and won't want to talk to me anyway."

"Get the wine glasses out, please, the ones with fluted stems. And do at least *try* to be sensible. It's really time you learned more social awareness. It'll be good for you to meet a nice young man like Marcus. He'll be a bit different from the boys you meet at school, no doubt."

Ruth watched her mother deftly folding white linen napkins into fan shapes. "There's nothing wrong with the boys at school," she retorted. "You haven't even met them, so how can you judge?"

"There was that tongue-tied individual who came round with the cat," her mother reminded her. "Not really the sort of boy I'd like to think of you associating with. Quite unsuitable."

"Unsuitable for what?"

"Oh, you know what I mean, Ruth. Stop being difficult. Perhaps you could finish laying the table for me after you've changed. And I do expect you to make an effort this evening."

Ruth trailed upstairs. She washed and changed,

brushed her hair and put on pearl earrings, frowning at her neat pale features in the dressing-table mirror. She looked like a demure, well-brought-up young girl, she thought – completely boring. Marcus would probably think she was about thirteen. She went downstairs to sort out cutlery, finishing just in time for the guests' prompt arrival.

"Virginia! How lovely to see you after all this time!" Mrs Heyford rose from the passenger seat of the sleek maroon car and wavered across the drive in her high heels.

Ruth's mother clasped her affectionately and kissed her cheek. "Judith! You look so well. And Keith – how are you?"

Ruth stood in the entrance hall, eyeing Mrs Heyford's short mink jacket with distaste. Mr Heyford – Keith – was shaking hands with her father, and a tall, conservatively-dressed youth was getting out of the back seat of the car. He had an unseasonable tan, and dark hair cut very short at the back and sides, with a long wavy fringe which flopped into his eyes; *quite suitable* for practising her social awareness on, Ruth thought cynically. Marcus, presumably, didn't need any practice.

"Ruth, darling!" She found herself enveloped in a fragrant hug. "How you've grown! You must have been in ankle socks last time we saw you."

Ruth smiled dutifully, unable to think of any sensible reply.

"And I expect you remember Marcus."

"Yes, slightly." They shook hands formally.

Minutes later Ruth found herself seated on the chintz sofa next to Marcus, who, with very little prompting, launched into a monologue about his recent skiing holiday, mentioning the names of several celebrities who'd been staying at the same resort. He didn't seem to expect Ruth to contribute to the conversation. Aware of her silence and her mother's disapproving glances, she was greatly relieved when they were finally summoned to sit at the table.

"You sit next to Marcus, Ruth," her mother told her. "And Keith, over here next to me."

"Pâté – my favourite," said Judith, noticing the plate in front of her.

Ruth looked at her own plate suspiciously. "What kind is it?" she asked her father.

"Pâté de foie gras."

Ruth poked at the heavy substance with her fork. She took a reluctant mouthful, remembering Melanie's words: "Pâté de foie gras – it's an obscenity. There are people starving for want of grain, while geese are being tortured and force-fed with the stuff to produce something that's supposed to be a *delicacy*. It'd choke me to eat it." Ruth tried to swallow, the richness cloying in her mouth. She put her fork down, unintentionally catching her father's eye.

"Don't you like it, darling?"

"I'm sorry, I can't eat it. It's too rich, after fasting," Ruth explained.

"It's delicious," Marcus said, balancing a loaded fork.

"Besides, I hate the thought of it,' Ruth plunged on recklessly, "those poor geese being force-fed. My friend Melanie's made her parents take it off the menu at their restaurant."

Her mother's eyes met hers in a meaningful glare across the table. "Just leave the pâté, darling," she said crisply. "This is hardly the time for a lecture." She turned to Judith. "I'm afraid some of Ruth's friends at the comprehensive are giving her radical ideas," she said apologetically.

"Oh dear, that is rather a worry," Judith sympathised. "I'm glad to say we haven't had any problems of that kind with Marcus. What a pity Ruth had to leave her old school."

Ruth bit back an indignant retort. Instead, she said calmly, "I think it did me good to change schools. And there's nothing radical about fund-raising for Oxfam, is there? Some of my friends are planning to do a sponsored parachute jump to raise money for famine relief."

"How marvellous," Judith said soothingly. "I do like to see young people doing something to help others."

"A chap I know does free-fall. Says it's an absolutely amazing experience," Marcus said. "His father's got his own plane. They've offered to take me up some time. I might be interested in doing a bit of sky-diving."

Ruth, stifling a wish for Marcus to do a jump without a parachute, lapsed into an offended silence while the others finished their first course. She went into the kitchen to help her father with the plates and the vegetable dishes, glad to escape from the superior Marcus and his condescending mother, even for a few moments.

She said little during the main course, toying with her casseroled beef. Marcus, obviously giving up on her, turned in his seat to talk to her father, on his other side, about a holiday he proposed to take in Scotland with a friend from school: "We should be able to get in a bit of shooting, and of course fishing."

Ruth listened sceptically. So this was her mother's idea of a suitable male companion, was it? An arrogant socialite who treated her with condescension and went round killing things in his spare time? Ruth remembered her mother's earlier remark about Jon being tongue-tied and *quite unsuitable*. If only she could see beyond outward appearances, she'd realize that Jon was worth ten of Marcus.

Seven

Chris was glad that his mother was still upstairs in her dressing gown, doing something to her hair, when the old white Talbot drew up outside, and was unlikely to appear.

He opened the front door. His father stood there by himself, looking edgy.

"Hello, Dad. Mum's upstairs in the bathroom."

His father's relief was obvious. "Lucy's waiting in the car."

Chris ushered Ian out of the front door and followed his father towards the car, feeling ridiculously nervous. The woman in the passenger seat got out as they approached, and said "Hello," rather shyly.

Chris, taken aback by her appearance, tried not to let his surprise show as he returned her greeting and got into the back seat. When his father had told him that Lucy was a good bit younger than he was, Chris had pictured someone glamorous and fashionably dressed. Lucy was small and slim, hardly bigger than Ian, with plain features and straight dark hair parted in the middle and falling to chin length, with a wispy fringe. She wore what looked like a man's Shetland sweater, a checked cotton shirt, cord jeans and lace-up shoes. Chris thought she looked drab, wondering what on earth his father saw in her.

"Where are we going, Dad?" Ian asked, fastening his seat-belt as the car pulled away.

"To the coast, near Eastbourne."

"I hope you're good at map-reading, Chris," Lucy said, turning in her seat to speak to him. "Jeff's asked me to navigate, and I'm hopeless at it." Her voice was pleasant, low-pitched, with a hint of a Welsh accent.

"I thought we'd take the country lanes, rather than head straight down the A-roads. There are some lovely villages," Jeff explained.

Lucy showed Chris the proposed route on the map, and passed round a packet of mints. When they were clear of the suburban estates and driving through farm land and villages, Jeff suggested playing Pub Sign Cricket, Ian's favourite car game. Chris guessed that his father had suggested this as a deliberate tactic, in case conversation proved difficult. In fact, he was relieved that Lucy didn't ask him any of the typical questions adults often felt compelled to ask, "What are you going to do when you leave school?" or "What do you do in your spare time?" She seemed content to gaze out of the window, helping Ian to spot pub signs, and to study her map, once or twice conferring with Chris. He noticed that she and his father occasionally looked at each other and exchanged smiles. He wondered how they behaved when they were alone together, finding it hard to imagine. Were they having an *affair*? Chris somehow couldn't reconcile the idea with someone as plain and unglamorous as Lucy.

"Can we go in the amusement arcades?" Ian asked when the Pub Sign Cricket had petered out.

"I shouldn't think so, not today," his father replied. "The weather's too fine to spend time indoors."

Chris wondered what he had in mind, hoping he wouldn't suggest looking round some dreary old castle or stately home. It was too cold for the beach, but a fine spring day, the sun shining hazily through the remnants of an early mist. The stunted trees in the orchards were still bare, but daffodils and crocuses brightened cottage gardens, and Lucy pointed out tiny lambs in the fields. Gradually the rich Wealden clay was replaced by the chalkier soil of the South Downs, and then there was the sea in front of them: calm, steely blue-grey, with a strip of reflected gold near the horizon, and humped hills undulating away to the west like the coils of the Loch Ness Monster rising from the sea.

"They're called the Seven Sisters," Jeff told Ian, pointing. "We'll have lunch first, then walk along. I hope it stays fine; there's cloud building up."

A picnic lunch was produced from the car boot. Chris felt rather touched by the care with which his father had planned the day, choosing the boys' favourite things to eat. Afterwards, they put on jackets and set out along the close-cropped turf over the switchback hills. It was sharply cold after the warmth of the car, the air as fresh as iced water.

Where the hill was at its highest, Chris walked as close as he dare to the cliff edge, where the chalk face sheered off dizzyingly below and gulls wheeled and screamed above. He imagined stepping off the edge into that terrifying drop, the sense of nothing but space beneath his feet. He turned to shout at his father, into the wind, "How high are these cliffs?"

"Beachy Head's four hundred and fifty feet. Probably about a hundred less than that, here." He waited for Chris to catch up, the wind tugging at his hair.

Chris wondered what it would be like to step out into nothing from two thousand feet. Perversely, he had been determined to do the parachute jump until his mother had finally agreed to give him permission; now that she had, and he felt committed to do it, he felt a surge of panic whenever he thought about it. Yet, at the same time, he knew that he would be disappointed if for some reason he were unable to do the jump. He told his father about Melanie's plans.

Jeff was impressed. "Good for you, if you're brave enough to do it – I'm not sure I would be. You can put me down for a fiver. Your mother's agreed to it, has she?"

"Yes. She took a bit of persuading, but she came round in the end."

"It's a terrific idea for fund-raising; should bring in a lot of money. You know," Jeff continued thoughtfully, "your friend Melanie's an unusual girl. Interesting."

"Melanie? Yes, she's all right." Chris was surprised, never really having thought of her as a girl, let alone an interesting one. He had known her for so long that she was just Melanie. To be interesting to Chris, a girl had to be pretty and feminine and shapely, like Lisa, or Ruth. The thought reminded him that he'd made little progress with Ruth. She'd seemed suspicious and guarded when he'd talked to her on the night of the Fast. He'd have to try harder, or he'd lose his bet.

A sudden shout made him look along the cliff path where Lucy and Ian had walked on ahead, two small figures side by side against the grey sky. A black Labrador lolloped up to them, ignoring its owner's cries. It bounded playfully from side to side, pink tongue panting, then jumped up at Lucy, placing muddy paws on her shoulders. She recovered her balance, patting the dog and laughing. The green hooded anorak she wore, with a scarlet scarf and gloves, made her look rather like a pixie. Chris thought she could hardly be more different from his mother, who would have made a fuss about the paw marks and complained about people not keeping their dogs under control. But then, she wouldn't have wanted to come on a walk like this anyway; if forced to go, she would have minced along in unsuitable shoes and then complained that her feet hurt.

"It's starting to rain." Ian held a hand out as Chris and his father caught up, and looked up at the darkening sky. "And we're a long way from the car."

"There's a café along here somewhere, if I remember rightly," Jeff said, turning up his coat collar as the first heavy drops began to fall. "We'll shelter there if it gets any heavier."

The rain storm began in earnest as they reached the exposed summit of the next hill. Abruptly, any semblance of a spring day vanished as the sleety rain drove into their faces. They ran, huddled into their coats, slipping and skidding on the wet chalk.

"There it is," Jeff panted, pointing to a cluster of low buildings near the shore. "There are a few cars parked – I hope that means it's open."

They dashed for the porch, crowding inside gratefully and shaking the rain from their anoraks. Jeff put an arm round Lucy's shoulders, steering her through the inner door. Chris watched as she pushed her hood back, looking up at Jeff, her face flushed from running and lit with a smile that gave her a quite unexpected beauty.

Ian, alerted by a bleeping sound, went straight to a video game by the counter, fed a coin into the machine and began zapping excitedly, while the others took their drinks to a window seat overlooking the rain-lashed sea. Chris clasped his cold hands round his mug of tea and grinned across the table at his father, nodding towards Ian. "That's made his day."

Jeff grinned back. His dark hair, beaded with rain,

was sticking to his forehead in damp curls; his face was free from the strain Chris had seen etched there in worried lines. Chris couldn't remember when he had last seen his father look so relaxed and happy. He looked out of the streaming window at the grey sea, oblivious of his wet feet and damp jeans, filled with a sense of deep contentment.

Gary had woken in a sweat of fear, his heart pounding. He gazed wildly around as the familiar shape of his bedroom window came slowly into focus. The dream was vivid in his mind – he was standing at the open doorway of a plane, looking out at the terrifying drop beneath. He was trying to explain to Melanie, who stood behind him, that he had no parachute, but no words would come out. Melanie just laughed and gave him a friendly push out into space.

He had seemed to leave the plane in slow motion, trying to make flying movements with his arms, still desperately trying to shout to the unconcerned Melanie . . . his head reeled as he fell. The sickening feeling of dizziness stayed with him after he had opened his eyes, and he put out a hand to make sure of the comforting solidity of his bed.

"It will be all right," he told himself. "Nothing can go wrong. Thousands of people jump out of aeroplanes every year. I'm more likely to have an accident riding my bike." But he couldn't rid himself of the cold clutch of fear in his stomach whenever he thought of the parachute jump.

At breakfast he looked at his parents with silent reproach. Why had they agreed so easily to him doing the jump? Didn't they care that their only son might plunge to his death? Gary's imagination ran on morbidly, composing his obituary for the local paper. "He was a popular boy, well-liked by everyone who knew him. His Headmaster said yesterday, 'It's a great loss to the school' ..."

Gary had tried to put a certain amount of hesitation into his voice when telling his parents about the proposed jump, but they had simply said, "As long as it's all properly organized, and Mr Scanlon's going with you," (as if Mr Scanlon were Superman, and could come swooping through the skies to snatch Gary to safety) and had signed the consent form. Their trouble, Gary thought, remembering discussions on sexual stereotyping in English at school, was that they expected boys to be macho and physical and daring. Gary usually did, too, but now he looked with envy at his little sister, who sat at the table pretending to feed her doll with cornflakes. It was all right for girls; they didn't have to prove themselves – not in that kind of way, at any rate. But then Gary remembered that Melanie was a girl, and that she seemed to be contemplating the parachute jump without any qualms at all.

After breakfast Gary decided to go swimming, feeling the need for physical exercise. Parking his bike by the Sports Centre, he was surprised to see Jon walking up to the entrance with a rolled towel, and even more surprised when Jon, ahead of him in the queue, produced a season ticket instead of paying ninety pence like everyone else.

"Watcha, Shirley," Gary said, catching up with Jon in the changing rooms. "Didn't know you were a regular swimmer."

"Yes, I've been coming every day," Jon told him.

"Every day? You aiming for the Olympics or something?"

"No. It's part of my plan to lose weight," Jon said shortly.

Gary knew that Jon was fed up with being teased about his diet. He had taken a fair part in the teasing, himself. However, when he saw Jon in his swimming trunks, he had to admit that the diet was having some effect. Jon was still – well, large, but considerably less flabby than Gary could remember him. You had to give old Shirley full marks for determination, Gary conceded, following Jon through the footbath.

He walked round to the deep end, his glance drawn towards a shapely girl in a red swimsuit with a deeply plunging back. He was pleased that the girl gave him an appreciative look in return. Gary was proud of his hard, muscular body, and if he were honest, part of the attraction of the swimming pool was the opportunity it gave of showing off his physique to admiring females. For the benefit of the girl in the red suit, he performed his most dashing racing dive, enjoying the

93

shock of the cool water and the thrust of his launch from the poolside. He surfaced, eyes stinging with chlorine, and propelled himself forward with powerful crawl strokes.

Ahead of him, Jon was swimming across the pool in a purposeful breaststroke. Gary made a mental note that if Jon could do such a good breaststroke as that, it might be worth including him in the form's swimming team next term. He grinned at the thought. Normally Shirley would be the last person to consider for any sporting event.

Gary completed his routine of ten lengths' front crawl and five lengths' back crawl, weaving in and out of the splashing children at the shallow end. As he finished and clung, panting, to the side, he glanced towards the diving boards at the deep end, where a stocky figure – yes, it was definitely Jon – was carefully climbing the ladder at the side. Gary watched, fascinated, as Jon passed the middle board and continued up to the top. Surely Jon wasn't going to dive off the top board? Gary, for all his prowess at swimming, had never ventured on to the boards, apart from the low springboard. Jon, reaching the top, walked to the edge and stepped off without hesitation, entering the water smoothly, feet first and arms raised, only a widening circle of ripples showing where he had been. Gary watched as he surfaced, conscious of surprise and admiration mixed with anxiety – he felt that Jon's feat was a challenge to himself.

"Christ, if old Shirley can do it, I must be able to,"

he told himself, striking out for the deep end steps. "It's not like diving in."

He got out of the pool and climbed the ladder resolutely until he reached the middle board. Clutching the hand-rail firmly, he made himself continue, trying to avoid looking down past his bare feet to the white tiles below. He reached the broad, canvas-covered surface of the top board, and walked towards the edge with hesitant steps. The hand-rail only went half-way along the board. He felt exposed as he crept nearer the edge, looking at the dizzying perspective beneath; the black lines on the pool's bottom wavered alarmingly. A swimmer came into sight beneath the projecting edge of board. Gary's toes clenched round the edge like fingers, his knees trembling as his dream came back to him, horribly vivid.

"But I've got to jump now," he thought. "I can't feebly go back down the steps."

He felt as if he would topple forwards. Before he was conscious of having made a decision, his right foot stepped out, the board vanished and he was plummeting down, the pale blue water rushing to meet him. He hit the surface with a force that smacked his legs and knocked the breath out of his body. He was deep under the water, frighteningly deep, bubbles rushing upwards, the surface far above him marked by a pair of thrashing legs. He kicked desperately; his downward progress slackened and levelled off, and he was rising, his lungs bursting and his ears pulsing with the pressure. He clawed at the water, and his head broke the surface at last. He gasped at the air, filling his lungs gratefully.

"Oi, you!" The pool guard was shouting at him from the side. "Look before you jump, you moron! You nearly landed on that little boy!"

"Sorry," Gary managed to gasp. He hadn't enough breath to explain that he hadn't exactly made a decision to jump; his feet had done it of their own accord. The pool guard turned away, tutting, and obviously thinking that Gary was a brainless lout.

The girl in the red swimsuit was standing by the pool guard, laughing at something he'd just said to her. Gary swam away, crushed and demoralized, trying to get his breathing back to normal.

"There's plenty of ready meals in the freezer – you can do yourself something in the microwave for lunch. We probably won't be back until five or six. Bye, darling."

Ruth stood in the porch and watched until her parents had driven out of sight. They'd been invited for Sunday lunch with her mother's new partner. Ruth, not interested in the prospect of food herself, didn't know how they could set out to eat several courses of lunch so soon after the extravagant meal of the night before. She knew how Melanie must feel, working in the restaurant and seeing the quantities of food wasted every night.

The day stretched emptily ahead of Ruth as she went unwillingly back into the big house. Homework, the Sunday papers, her violin practice; she had things to do, but none of them suited her mood. She felt restless, and for some reason she kept thinking of Jon, seeing his wistful face as he watched her across the room on the night of the Fast. Jon had been kind to her, overcoming his shyness, and she knew that she'd hurt him by ignoring him. She felt that it was up to her to put things right.

There was a simple solution to her problem: why not go and see him now, and tell him why she'd been so off-hand? She quickly rejected the idea as stupid, but it wouldn't go away. She knew roughly where he lived: near where she'd met him with the cat. And there was always the 'phone book. She leafed through the pages. S for Shirley – yes, there was only one Shirley listed: 8 Farringdon Walk. She passed the end of Farringdon Walk each week on her way to and from her violin lesson.

She fetched her coat, checked that she had her front-door key, and set off purposefully. By the time she reached Farringdon Walk, a street of terraced houses with neat front gardens, her pace had slowed to a reluctant dawdle, but she forced herself to walk up the path of No.8, and rang the doorbell.

The door was opened by a stout woman in a flowered PVC apron.

"Hello. I'm sorry to bother you. Is Jon in?" Ruth asked politely.

"Gone swimming, love. He'll be back any minute. You can come in and wait for him, if you like."

"Thanks, but I . . ."

"Come on in, love, and have a cup of coffee. Jon won't be long, and I was just making a cup for me and Dad." Mrs Shirley ushered Ruth inside before she could protest. She found herself in a small, comfortable sitting room, where Monty, the indirect cause of her visit, sat propped up panda-like on a large flowered sofa, licking the white expanse of his chest.

"Sit down, love. I'll put the kettle on."

Ruth sat down next to Monty and stroked him, but he refused to be distracted from his washing. There was an appetizing smell of roasting potatoes and gravy. She hoped the Shirleys weren't just about to have lunch; she'd forgotten all about the time. It was nearly half-past twelve, according to a clock on the mantelpiece. The room, with its loudly ticking clock and comforting smells, reminded Ruth of visits to her grandmother. There was a bowl of yellow crocuses on a small table by the window, and a framed photograph of Jon in his school uniform, apparently being presented with some sort of prize.

Mrs Shirley reappeared with coffee cups on a tray. "Dad's in the garden; he'll be in in a minute. You must be the young lady our Monty scratched. Jon was quite upset about that. How are you finding school, love? It must have been hard for you, changing schools with your exams coming up. Sugar?"

"I like the school, now. No sugar, thank you." Ruth wondered just what Jon had told his mother about her, and why. Mrs Shirley was like Jon in some ways, large and comfortable, with kind grey eyes, like her son's, and dark wavy hair with an untidy fringe, like his.

"Has that Melanie got you involved in all this fund-raising?" Mrs Shirley asked, passing a plate of biscuits.

"Yes. I did the Sponsored Fast last week."

At that point the front door could be heard opening and then Jon came into the room, carrying his rolled towel, his hair still damp from swimming. His eyes opened wide with amazement as he saw Ruth sitting on the sofa.

"Hello, love. Have a good swim?" his mother asked, unperturbed. "Ruth and I are just having a nice chat."

"Oh . . . er . . . hello, Ruth." Jon wondered why his mother offered no explanation for Ruth's being there. He wasn't sure what to say; "What are you doing here?" would sound a bit blunt.

"My parents have gone out for the day," Ruth began.

"What, and left you all on your own?" Mrs Shirley interrupted, as if Ruth were six years old. "No wonder you're feeling lonely. You're an only child, are you, like Jon? Why don't you stay and have dinner with us? There's plenty to go round."

Ruth had already found out that Mrs Shirley simply didn't listen to refusals of offers of hospitality. In spite of her protests – "Thank you, that's very kind, but I really couldn't ..." – she was soon seated at the table with Jon and his father, who had greeted her with a firm handshake and a sort of knowing look, while Mrs Shirley bustled about in the kitchen.

"I hate to think of you going back to an empty house, love," Mrs Shirley said, carrying in a steaming joint of beef, "and we've plenty, with Jon on this diet. He hardly eats enough for a sparrow."

Jon, passing Ruth the dish of roast potatoes, was acutely aware of the difference between her home and his. What on earth must she think of his dad in shirtsleeves and muddy trousers straight from the garden, and his mum who must be about twenty years older than hers, and who rarely stopped talking to let anyone else get a word in? To say nothing of the house itself, which must look to Ruth like something in a museum, compared with her own Ideal Home surroundings. His parents had found out that Ruth came from Gloucestershire, and were reminiscing about visits to the Cotswolds: "What's the name of that place with the river running through it, and the model village? That's right, love, Bourton-on-the-Water. I remember stopping there once with Gran. And there's Chipping Campden – that's a lovely town ... we went to Hidcote Manor once on a coach trip, do you remember that, Jon, those lovely gardens ...?"

Slowly it dawned on Jon that Ruth was enjoying herself, joining in the conversation animatedly, and accepting a second helping of apple-pie. He began to relax. His parents liked Ruth, he could see; she was what they thought of as a nicely brought-up young lady. He wished it wasn't quite so obvious that they thought she was his girlfriend. He'd have to explain after she'd left. And he still didn't even know why she'd come round.

"Thank you so much for asking me to stay. It was a lovely meal and I've really enjoyed meeting you," Ruth told the Shirleys later, after helping with the washing-up.

"Come again, love. We'll be pleased to see you any time."

"I'll walk home with you," Jon offered. He fetched her jacket and held it out while she put it on. As they left, he pictured his parents exchanging pleased looks. "Well! Who would have thought our Jon could find himself a nice young lady like that!" He rather wished they were right in their assumption. But by now Chris had probably asked Ruth out, and she'd soon be potty about him, if she wasn't already. He was dying to know.

"I hope you didn't mind – you know, Mum practically forcing you to stay," he remarked instead.

Ruth looked startled. "Of course I didn't mind! Your parents are so *kind*. It was lovely. I hope *you* didn't mind."

"Of course not." There was a pause. Jon's thoughts were racing. If it wasn't for the fact that he was certain Chris was going out with Ruth, he would have suggested another meeting – after all, he wouldn't be likely to have a better opportunity. He thought she was lovely, completely without affectation, and amazingly it did seem that she liked him after all.

"I had a really awful evening last night," Ruth said suddenly. "Some ghastly friends of my parents came to dinner, with a horrible son called Marcus, and I had to try and talk to him. He was so stuck-up and conceited, I felt like strangling him."

"What made you come round to the house this morning?" Jon finally got out the question he'd been wanting to ask. "Did you just happen to be passing, or what?"

The answer came to Ruth in a flash of brilliance.

"I wanted to ask you to teach me to play chess," she said.

Later that evening Ruth answered the phone, expecting the call to be from one of her parents.

"Hello?"

"Hello, Ruth? This is Chris."

There was a pause while Ruth adjusted her thoughts. *Chris.* She suspected that she was the source of some joke shared by Chris and Gary; she'd noticed Gary's look of eager amusement when Chris had asked her to help him with his maths, and something in Chris's manner which suggested that he was confident no female could possibly resist him.

"Hello, Chris," she said guardedly.

102

"I was just wondering if you're doing anything next Friday night. I'm going to a party and I thought you might come with me."

There was another pause.

"Thanks, it's kind of you to ask, but I'm doing something else on Friday night."

Eight

At the end of PE on Monday, Jon was about to leave the changingroom when he noticed Gary sitting in a corner by himself, looking dejected.

"What's the matter, Gary? Are you ill?"

Gary was making no effort to get changed, but was sitting slumped forward on to his knees, looking rather green.

"I'm not ill," Gary moaned. "I just feel sick, that's all."

Jon was confused. "Well, that's ill, isn't it?"

"If you really want to know, I mean sick with fear."

It was so rare for the usually extrovert Gary to be downcast that Jon felt certain he must be really ill.

"Sick with fear? What are you frightened of?"

"Of the parachute jump, of course," Gary mumbled. "I feel terrified whenever I think of it. I was terrified at the swimming pool, when I went up on the top board. And in the gym just now, I made myself go all the way to the top of the wall bars. I nearly fell off with fright, and my hands were so sweaty I could hardly hold on. I'm just not good with heights. I'm petrified of going up in planes, even. I'll probably have hysterics and do something stupid and kill myself."

"Well, no-one can blame you for being scared. I should think anyone'd be scared, even Mr Scanlon. You'd be stupid if you *weren't* scared."

"No, it's worse than that," Gary insisted. "It's a kind of phobia. You know, how some people have a dread of being shut in lifts, or of spiders or the dark or whatever. With me it's heights."

"Well, don't do the jump then. You can drop out – excuse the pun."

Gary managed a weak grin. "But how can I not do it? Everyone'll know I've bottled out, and I've already got loads of sponsors. And besides, Melanie's doing it – a *girl* – " Gary's voice trailed off hopelessly.

Jon was silent, thinking it over. He was amazed to learn that Gary was afraid of heights – tough, athletic Gary, who was in all the school sports teams. He was brilliant at football and swimming and weight-lifting and running and any other kind of physical activity – except rock-climbing, Jon remembered; Gary hadn't gone on the recent trip to Bowles Rocks. Jon was scared of heights himself, but no-one would be surprised about that. He could understand what loss of face it would entail to admit defeat, especially for someone with Gary's reputation. And, after all, he hadn't chosen to do the jump in the first place; he'd been more or less forced into it.

"We'll have to think of some way for you not to do it – for someone else to do it instead," Jon said at length. "You could sprain your ankle or something, playing football. You couldn't possibly jump then."

"That'd look a bit suspicious, wouldn't it?"

"Maybe. But you could fall over on the football field in front of everyone and come off limping. That'd make it look fairly realistic. I'll trip you up myself, if you like."

"But what about all my sponsors?"

'Whoever else does the jump will have to take them over. Make sure you get sponsors from school, not aunts and uncles and that sort of thing. Then it won't matter much who actually jumps."

"Hmm." Gary started to get dressed, beginning to look more like his usual self. "I shall feel awful, if someone else jumps instead of me. But not as bad as I would if I had to do it myself."

"There's no need to feel awful," Jon said consolingly. "There are plenty of things you're good at. No-one can expect you to be able to do everything."

"Well, thanks for your idea." Gary shrugged himself into his shirt and paused. "And Jon – you won't let on, will you? I mean, Chris is actually looking forward to it – I'd hate it if he knew . . ."

"Of course I won't."

Gary buttoned up his shirt, feeling a bit more cheerful. He realized that he needn't have asked Jon to keep quiet. Jon would have kept his secret anyway.

* * *

"I've marked your Thomas Hardy essays," Ms Vine said, producing a sheaf of papers from her brief-case. "They're going in your folders as a major text assignment, so I'm pleased most of you did so well with them. There were one or two surprises – " she sorted through the batch of essays and waved one at the class – "this one, for example. It's yours, Chris. I gave you about two grades higher than you usually get. Your essay showed such a genuine, strong personal response that I'd like to read some of it out to the class."

She didn't ask him if he minded having it read out, and Chris had to sit there feeling like a wally while she read out the piece he'd written about "The Roman Gravemounds", the poem about the man burying his dead cat. Lisa, recovering from her exaggerated astonishment at hearing Chris singled out for praise in an English lesson, began to sniff and to mime wiping tears away from her eyes. He hit her leg under the table to make her shut up. He'd face more teasing about it later, he knew.

When Ms Vine gave the essay back to him, he looked at the angular green writing at the end: *Well done, Chris – you've chosen an interesting range of poems and have shown your response to them very clearly, as well as making detailed comments on style. This is very promising indeed. B++.* Chris felt rather pleased, in spite of the embarrassment. He'd never realized before that it was so easy to get a good grade in English – he'd liked that poem, so he'd read it carefully and simply written down what he felt about it, and why he thought some of the descriptions and contrasts worked well.

"A lousy D –, as usual," Lisa muttered beside him. She passed her essay over to Chris, and he read the comment: *This really isn't sufficient, Lisa. It's not enough simply to choose a few poems and say what each one's about. You're not translating from a foreign language.* "And after I went to all that trouble to get it finished on time, for once," Lisa continued. 'You'd better tell me how it's done. I never knew you were into poetry and all that poofter stuff."

Lisa was in one of her spiky moods, in which nothing pleased her. Chris had arranged to meet her later that evening, to go to the cinema. By the time they were sitting together on the top deck of the bus, however, he was wishing he hadn't bothered. Lisa had kept him waiting at her house, because she said her hair was a mess and she couldn't get it to look right, so they were already late; then she'd complained about having to wait for buses, telling Chris that her previous boyfriend, who was eighteen, had his own car. Something in her tone reminded Chris of his mother.

"And my Mum didn't want me to come out tonight," she grumbled as the bus pulled into the town centre. "She said I should catch up with my coursework so that I don't have to spend all the Easter holidays doing it."

Chris knew that Lisa never took the slightest bit of notice of what her mum wanted her to do, especially if it involved doing homework. He was about to challenge her, "Well, why did you come then?" when Lisa suddenly pointed out of the window.

"There's Melanie! Where d'you reckon she's going?"

Chris looked out of the window. Melanie, in jeans and a black quilted coat, was walking down the side street which led to the Friends' Meeting House.

"I know where she's going. To a meeting of the local Oxfam group. She told me this morning."

Lisa gave a derisive laugh. "An Oxfam meeting! Doesn't that girl ever think of anything else? Still, I suppose it's the only way she gets any social life."

"What do you mean?"

Lisa didn't notice the warning note in his voice.

"Well, look at the fat cow. Who'd be seen dead with her? I don't know why she doesn't do something with herself. Okay, she'll never be pretty, but at least she could lose some weight and do something with her hair and get some decent clothes. And she's so bloody *bossy*, with all her stupid fasts and parachute jumps. I suppose it's the only way she can get boys to take any notice of her. She ought to team up with Jon. They'd make a good pair."

She sat slumped back in her seat, her eyes a-light with malicious interest. Chris turned on her, furious.

"Who the bloody hell do you think you are?" he demanded. "Who are you to criticize Melanie? You think you're so bloody irresistible, don't you? It doesn't occur to you that you ought to be *nice* to people."

Lisa was staring at him in amazement. "What's bugging you? What's it to you what I say about Melanie?"

"I'll tell you what's bugging me," Chris continued in a voice tight with suppressed anger. "At least Melanie *does* something, she's not totally negative like you, always moaning and complaining. She's – " he paused, remembering what his father had said " – *interesting*. But you can't see that, can you? All you can see is that she doesn't fit the – the stereotype of how you think a girl ought to look and behave. You think that's all there is to it, looking right." He searched his brain for some final insult. "You're so sure of yourself, thinking you're better than her. But compared with her, you are totally, completely, mind-blowingly, *boring*." He stood up, oblivious of interested stares from other passengers. "You can go to the pictures by yourself, if you want. I don't want to go anywhere with you again."

He stomped along the top deck of the bus and down the steps in a magnificently dramatic exit. As the bus drew up at the traffic lights, he jumped down and strode off down the High Street, hands thrust deep in his jacket pockets, the evening breeze cooling his face. He was still furious, remembering the smug, self-confident tone in Lisa's voice. She'd been temporarily struck dumb with surprise at his outburst; he knew how angry she'd be, not to have had the last word, to

110

have been left sitting there open-mouthed in front of all those passengers. He kicked at an empty Coke can lying on the pavement, and watched it ricochet satisfyingly round a bus shelter. Where he was going now, he had no idea; he didn't want to go home yet, he just wanted to walk for a bit, by himself.

He thought of what he'd said to Lisa. It had sounded great; he'd impressed himself with the way the words had just spilled out. But the truth of his words came home to him now in a quite unexpected way. When it came to what he'd said to her about appearances and all that, wasn't he just as bad as her? He'd encouraged her, really; he knew what she was like, that she wasn't a nice person at heart, and yet he'd wanted to go out with her. He knew the reason, if he was honest – he liked going out with a girl who was generally admired and lusted after. At the moment, he didn't feel very proud of himself for that. It was all very well *saying* that appearances weren't important, but he'd been brought up with his mother's values; he'd learned from her that they were. Phrases drifted into his mind, things she had shouted at Jeff: "For God's sake, why do you have to let yourself go like this? Do you think I'm going out with you dressed like that? What will people think?" She'd always taught Chris to present himself well, and he didn't see anything wrong with that. And yet, he knew now that he respected his father far more than his mother, that he preferred his father's values in life. As soon as he was old enough to choose for himself, he'd go to live with Jeff, if his father was willing to have him.

Chris had calmed down now, enough to be distracted by a display of record album covers in a shop window. He pictured Lisa's predicament, left there by herself at the front of the bus, with all those people staring at her. It was worth any future unpleasantness she might cause, just to have seen the look on her face; she deserved to be told a few home truths. God, it had been a marvellous moment! He grinned suddenly, seeing the funny side of his outburst.

On the Wednesday morning of the last week of term, Melanie came into the form-room looking distraught.

"It's this 'flu that's going round," she told Jon and Chris. "People are going down with it like flies. I've just come in with Gary, and he's practically lost his voice. That's how it starts. If he gets any worse, he won't be able to go on Saturday."

Ms Vine had been absent from school all week; a supply teacher had taken her lessons. On Tuesday, Gregory had gone home feeling ill at lunchtime, and Ruth had a slight sore throat, but nothing worse as yet. Now, Jon thought, fate looked like taking a hand to help Gary out of his predicament, giving him either the 'flu, or the chance to fake or exaggerate illness. It might not be necessary, after all, to stage a football accident. Jon rather hoped, for Gary's sake, that the 'flu would develop.

"We'll have to keep our fingers crossed Mr Scanlon doesn't get it," Melanie said. "If he's ill, we won't be able to go at all. And he's got nearly two hundred pounds promised in sponsor money, more than any of the rest of us."

By afternoon registration, Gary looked pale and said he was feeling dizzy; Mr Scanlon took him round to the school offices to be sent home. Even Jon, who knew of Gary's motives, couldn't tell whether he was genuinely ill or merely putting up a convincing performance.

"Don't *breathe* on him, Gary," Melanie whispered in anguish as they left the room.

"Now what?" Chris said. "Who's the likeliest person you can think of to do a parachute jump at short notice?"

"Don't look at me," said Balvinder hastily. "I told you, you wouldn't catch me doing it. Not after I read about that bloke who – "

"We don't want to know," Melanie interrupted.

"What happened to him?" Chris asked, curious.

"I'll tell you after Saturday," Balvinder said, catching Melanie's eye.

"Oh, come on, this isn't getting us anywhere." Melanie leaned her elbows on the table and pushed her hands through her springy hair with an air of desperation. "Who can we get to do the jump?"

"I'll do it," Jon said unexpectedly.

A stunned silence greeted this remark.

"Are you serious, Shirley?" Chris said at length,

quite unable to hide his astonishment.

"Yes. I want to do it."

"Really, Jon? That's fantastic." Melanie wasn't going to give him more than one chance to change his mind. She swept on, reaching into her bag, "Look, this is what you've got to do. I've got a spare set of forms; take them home tonight and read them all . . . "

"They won't let Jon jump," Lisa interrupted from the other side of the form-room. "He'd make a bloody great hole in the ground."

"Oh, shut up, Lisa," Chris said sharply. "Who asked you to stick your oar in? Jon's already done a damn sight more than you have towards the campaign. Go and bitch at someone else."

Melanie looked from Chris to Lisa and back again with interest, wondering what had happened between them. She handed the forms to Jon. "This one's the Consent Form. Get your parents to sign it and give them all back to me tomorrow morning."

Mr Scanlon's eyebrows shot up into his thick, wavy hair. "So Jon's really going instead?"

"Providing his parents agree."

"Well, good for him. It's a shame for Gary – he must be disappointed."

"Yes, he was, I think."

Chris had offered to help Mr Scanlon to take the video recorder on its trolley back to the cupboard

114

where it belonged, so that he could tell him the latest news.

"How much do we stand to make now, then?" Mr Scanlon asked, reaching into his pocket for the cupboard key.

"A hell of a lot. There's your two hundred pounds to start with, then Melanie's got a hundred and twenty. I'll get about seventy, and Gary had at least fifty which Jon can take over, and perhaps get some more of his own."

"That's well over four hundred pounds, then. Not bad at all."

"Yes," Chris said with satisfaction, "we should easily make more than the Fast. Melanie thought it might just about make three hundred and ninety, if everyone collected in what they said they would."

"You'll need to move that film projector first. That's right – put it on the shelf. But what does it matter whether the jump makes more than the Fast? It's all going to the same place in the end, isn't it?"

"Yes. It's just a sort of competition between me and Melanie. I know it sounds stupid, especially as she's doing the jump herself."

"Oh, well." Mr Scanlon locked the door, looking baffled. "I suppose it all helps to bring the money in. But what about the parachute course fees? Where's that money coming from?"

"Oh, sh – " Chris stopped himself just in time, remembering that Mr Scanlon was after all a teacher.

"I'd forgotten to take that into account. Do you mean they're going to beat us after all?"

"I'm glad there won't be room in Mr Scanlon's car for me to come and watch," Ruth said, walking home beside Jon. "I wouldn't dare. Honestly, I think you're so *brave*."

She'd told Jon several times already. Although it was flattering that she was so impressed, he felt she ought to reserve her admiration until he'd actually performed the jump.

"I'm not brave," he insisted. "I'll be absolutely rigid with fright."

"But you're still going to do it. *That's* what's brave."

Jon still wasn't quite sure what had prompted his sudden decision; he had spoken first and thought about it afterwards. Now he was having severe doubts, but one thing he was sure of – he couldn't back out now. To Ruth, one sentence had transformed him into a hero, a sort of latter-day Douglas Bader or Red Baron, daredevil of the air. Jon wasn't used to that sort of admiration, particularly from a girl, and particularly from a girl as nice as Ruth.

"Do you think your parents will agree to give you permission?" Ruth asked.

"Yes," Jon lied.

They wouldn't, he knew. One problem with having older-than-average parents was that they tended to be more cautious and protective than most; they weren't going to agree to let their only son and heir plunge out of an aeroplane two thousand feet above the ground. This did, of course, offer a chance of escape from the deal, but Jon had no intention of taking it.

At home, he read through the forms carefully, the insurance bits about death and injury giving him nasty qualms. You had to be over sixteen to do the jump – Jon's sixteenth birthday had been in December – and if you were under eighteen, your parents had to sign the Consent Form.

Jon wasn't above resorting to deception. While his parents were watching television, he took his mother's National Savings book from the letter rack in the kitchen where she kept it, and carefully copied her signature.

Nine

"*He jumped without a parachute from forty thousand feet*," Balvinder and some of the others had sung in a cheerful chorus at the end of school. Melanie found she was humming the tune now, as she went downstairs to wait for Mr Scanlon to pick her up. "*They scraped him off the runway like a dollop of strawberry jam, and he ain't gonna jump no more*." The words of the stupid song echoed in her head. She felt jittery with nerves, as if she were waiting for all the exams and dentist appointments of her whole life rolled into one; it didn't feel at all like the first day of the Easter holidays. Outside, the sky was still dark, with a pinkish glow near the horizon streaked with grey cloud; a breeze shook the bare branches of the ash tree in the front garden. Melanie knew that if the cloud thickened or the wind rose, there would be no parachuting.

Mr Scanlon arrived punctually at six-thirty, with Chris in the passenger seat of his car and Jon in the back.

"You're navigating, Chris." Mr Scanlon passed

over a road atlas and pointed out the route. "M25, M40, turn off here for Banbury, and the airfield is there – Hinton-in-the-Hedges."

"Fine," Chris said. "I've brought my camera," he told Melanie, "so I hope we can get some photos for the local paper."

"Oh, good. I forgot mine."

"I'm glad you agreed to stand in at the last minute, Jon," Mr Scanlon said. "I bet poor Gary's feeling fed up today. It was lucky your parents agreed to let you go, at such short notice."

Jon said nothing, and Melanie shot him a sidelong glance, her suspicions aroused.

"I hope you've had time to psych yourself up," Mr Scanlon continued. "The rest of us have had a couple of weeks to get used to the idea."

"You speak for yourself," Chris joked. "I don't think I'll get used to the idea till I'm flying through the air."

Jon felt awful about lying to his parents. He hadn't told them anything about Gary being ill, and had said that he was just going along with the others to watch, and to give moral support. He'd felt even worse when they hadn't suspected anything. He'd have to tell them before next week's local paper came out, if there were going to be photographs in it. They were making reasonable time, he saw, checking his watch as they headed up the M40; they should be in good time for the quarter-to-nine start. Mr Scanlon turned off the motorway and headed out along a country road, avoiding Banbury, which he said would be a bottle-neck.

"Nearly there now," Chris said. "This is Northamptonshire. We go through the next village, Farthinghoe, and then we turn off to the right."

The road they were on was rural, with views over undulating fields and woods, the verges thick with luxuriant spring growth, splashed in places with celandines. A signpost marked *Hinton Airfield* directed them into a narrow country lane which wound between hedges and past fields where black-and-white cows grazed. The lane, becoming little more than a track, led out into an open expanse of farmland, planted with crops.

"Is this it?" Melanie had expected the airfield to be something like Farnborough or Biggin Hill, with control towers and various kinds of planes dotted about, and pilots hurrying to and fro in flying suits and goggles. This place looked deserted, apart from a few cars parked in front of a cluster of farm buildings, and a hangar further along the perimeter track, with two tiny planes standing in front of it, looking like toys. A small, decaying brick-built lookout tower hinted at military origins.

"It's not a very big place, is it?" Chris remarked, looking around in surprise.

"A barn with blue doors, the instructor said. This must be it," Melanie confirmed, as Mr Scanlon pulled in and parked alongside the other cars.

As they got out, stretching stiff legs, the blue door

of the barn opened, and a smallish man dressed in a blue zipped overall came to meet them. "You must be the group from Kent," he said, smiling and shaking hands with each of them in turn. "I'm Mike Bolton, the Chief Instructor. Did you find your way all right?"

"Fine, thanks," Mr Scanlon told him.

Jon, following the others into the building, looked at Mike Bolton with relief. He'd vaguely expected some huge, muscle-bound SAS type, as hard as nails and with little sympathy for ordinary human failings. Mike Bolton was slightly built; he looked wiry and strong, but he had a kindly face with warm brown eyes, and a reassuring air of calm about him.

The inside of the barn was laid out like a classroom, with rows of chairs facing a blackboard and display board at one end. Trestle tables were lined up along the length of the building, and an orange-and-white parachute was spread out to cover the whole of the wall facing the chairs. A pin-board by the door was covered with newspaper cuttings. Four people were already seated on the chairs filling in forms.

"You've already done yours, haven't you?' said Mike Bolton. Melanie handed them over. "Got the parents' signatures – you're all under eighteen, aren't you, apart from your teacher, of course?"

"Yes, all in order," Mr Scanlon said.

Jon felt that his face would give him away. He

turned away, studying the newspaper cuttings on the notice board.

"Right. If you'd like to sit down, then, we'll start the first session," Mike said.

This consisted of an introductory talk about parachuting in general and the rules of the British Parachuting Association. "You'll do at least six hours training, probably more like eight. The cloud cover's too low for parachuting at the moment, less than two thousand feet, but if it lifts a bit you should be able to jump this evening."

Mike showed them a plan of the Drop Zone, a triangular section of the airfield, and then gave them a preliminary look at a parachute pack. Jon tried to conceal his alarm as Mike demonstrated how the static line, which would inflate the parachute under the weight of a falling body, was attached to the back of the pack in a series of loops. The thought that such a slim cord would be all that prevented him from crashing to his death was not encouraging.

"Does it really open by itself, every single time?" he asked Chris as they left the building at the end of the session.

"So they say. And you have a reserve parachute just in case it doesn't."

"Hmm. I suppose the chances of *both* parachutes failing to open must be fairly slim."

"Less than fairly slim, I hope," Chris agreed fervently. "I'm not sure about the idea of jumping off the plane *backwards*. It sounds pretty hairy to me."

"I know, and remembering to count. I'm sure I'll forget all about it."

The counting was what they had to practise next, after a coffee break in the stone farmhouse. Mike made them stand in a row outside the barn, bent forward, hands on knees, then jump backwards, arms and legs spread out and backs arched. "*One* thousand, *two* thousand, *three* thousand, *four* thousand, *CHECK CANOPY!*" they had to shout in unison. Melanie couldn't help wanting to giggle; she felt so silly, especially as some other people – experienced parachutists – had arrived and were standing watching, but she made herself concentrate. She could see that it was a way of overcoming your fears, schooling yourself to listen and obey Mike's shout of "*GO!*", and to follow the routine you'd had instilled into you. Mike made them do this about ten times before leading them back inside the barn and spreading mats out on the floor.

"Right. Now landing falls. We'll do side landings first."

He demonstrated a few times, making it look easy. With both arms held above his head as if holding parachute toggles, he bent slightly at the knees, then rolled sideways on to the mat, knees and feet neatly together all the while. It wasn't as simple as it looked, though; Melanie found that she wanted to put a hand down automatically to save herself as she fell.

"You mustn't do that," Mike reproved. "You could easily break a wrist."

She felt battered and bruised by the time Mike said they'd mastered sideways, backward and forward falls satisfactorily. Later, he told them, they'd jump from a table and go into a roll. They went back to the farmhouse for lunch, during which the pilot, a tall young man in a grey flying-suit, arrived and was introduced as Peter. After lunch, he and Mike took everyone out to look at the plane, which looked frighteningly small and frail, quivering slightly in the wind. It was a Cessna 180, white, with a red stripe along the side; the cockpit was tiny, with just one seat for the pilot and room for four others to crouch alongside and behind. The control panel reminded Melanie of an old-fashioned sports car. She looked anxiously towards Peter, reassured by his air of calm efficiency.

Mike had climbed into the cockpit and was crouching next to the pilot's seat to explain about aircraft drills.

"Right. This is the Number One position. When we're at two thousand feet and approaching the exit point, I'll tell you I'm about to open the in-flight door, and you'll feel a great whoosh of slipstream. Then I'll shout CUT! and when Peter slows down to seventy miles per hour, I'll tap you on the shoulder and shout EXIT. Then this is what you do."

Jon felt himself going pale with fright as he watched Mike calmly putting one foot out on to the little wooden step at the side of the plane. "The slipstream will really hit you then, so keep your weight well forward as you lean over the strut. Then change feet like this – " he demonstrated, left foot on the step, right leg extended out backwards " – and when I shout *GO*! you jump backwards with your left foot and throw yourself into the spread position, then you start counting."

He mentioned this as if it were as easy as getting off a bus. Jon's mind blanked out as he tried to imagine what it would be like, up there in the sky, stepping out with just that little wooden step between you and the ground. And what if you fell off . . . ?

"Okay, we'll just practise that a few times."

This practice was followed by more theory about canopy control, which meant steering the parachute in order to land as nearly as possible on target. Throughout the afternoon, Mike kept looking out of the window at the sky; the clouds were still hovering at around two thousand feet, so no definite plans could be made yet.

"It makes it worse, this indecision about the weather, doesn't it?" Chris said as they went round to the house for a tea break. "I'd really rather know we were definitely going to jump."

"Yes," Melanie agreed. "No matter how you think you're mentally geared up to do it, there's this little thought at the back of your mind that you might not have to after all."

* * *

Ruth had been thinking of the parachute jumpers all day. She wished now that she'd been able to go with them, to watch – she'd thought that would be bad, watching helplessly from the ground as they exposed themselves to what seemed to her to be terrible dangers, but it was infinitely worse to be at home while the hours of the day stretched out interminably, with nothing for her to do but wait. She felt quite incapable of turning her mind to anything else.

"If you've nothing better to do, Ruth, you might go into town for me," her mother said halfway through the afternoon. "I forgot to pick up a couple of things from the chemist."

"Okay."

In Boots, wandering through the aisles of shampoo and hairspray looking for the particular brand of conditioner specified by her mother, Ruth came suddenly face to face with Jon's mum.

"Hello, Mrs Shirley."

"Hello, Ruth, love! At home today, are you? I thought you'd have gone with the others up to Northamptonshire."

"No, there wasn't room in the car for spectators. Only for those who are actually doing the parachute jump."

"But Jon isn't doing the jump, love. He's just going to watch."

"But he – "

With a horrible shock, Ruth realized what Jon must have done, but it was too late to control her reaction, to stop her surprise from showing in her face.

Ten

The training was finished. They knew about aircraft drills, canopy control, hazardous landings, what to do if their main chute didn't open; they knew how to behave on the plane; they knew what to do with the parachute after landing; they'd done everything. Except jump.

The experienced parachutists were still waiting, hoping to do some free-fall jumping; they were fanatical, Melanie decided, prepared to wait hours for a jump lasting about two minutes. There had been occasional showers during the day, and dark clouds still hung obstinately over the airfield, giving tantalizing glimpses through to clear blue sky above.

"It'll lift. There's still time, a good couple of hours yet," Mike said confidently. "The evening is often the best time of day."

Melanie and Chris, to relieve the tension of waiting, walked down the perimeter road towards the hangars. A glider was coming in to land on the runway, its wings long and elegant like an albatross's. Evening was settling over the landscape, which undulated gently to the horizon, fields and hedges and woods as far as the eye could see; the small village of Hinton-in-the-Hedges, stone houses in a mantle of trees, lay huddled in a slight dip. Melanie tried to imagine what it would all look like from the air. Overhead, layers of grey cloud, like paint laid on a watercolour wash, blotted out the sun; beyond, the sky was blue, as smooth as parachute silk.

They sat down on a slab of stone, looking over the airfield in companionable silence. The breeze was cool in their faces, but Chris felt warmed with a sudden contentment. The waiting, nerve-racking though it was, heightened the feeling of anticipation.

"How will you feel if we can't jump tonight?" he asked Melanie.

"Relieved. Disappointed. I don't know which I'd feel most."

"You know, I love this place. This airfield is so *unmodern*, out here in the middle of all these cows and haystacks. It reminds me of World War One films, the feel of it." Chris looked around with satisfaction. He felt he wanted to say something to Melanie, almost to thank her. He turned to look at her. Her face was impassive, her strong features in profile, her dark wavy hair whipped into tendrils by the breeze; she was chewing thoughtfully on a stem of grass and looking into the distance. "You're not scared, are you?" he said, admiringly.

She turned to look at him, her hazel eyes amused. "Not scared? I'm bloody terrified!"

"Well, you're hiding it well. You know . . ." he paused, not sure what he wanted to say. "I can't think of any other girl who'd be out here doing this."

"Rubbish! There must be thousands of female parachutists."

"Yes, but think of people we know at school. Can you see Lisa parachuting?"

"Well, not Lisa, perhaps. But there's nothing special in me doing it. It's no different for me than for you. We'll both hit the ground just as hard."

Chris paused, Melanie's forthright response confounding him. He usually had no trouble talking to girls, but Melanie was different, even though he'd known her for so long; she swept flattery aside, taking everything he said absolutely seriously. He started again. "You know, I met my dad's girlfriend last weekend. I always hated the thought of Dad going out with someone – I suppose it's because I don't think anyone can be good enough for him. Anyway, I suppose I expected someone like my mum, you know, glamorous, trendy and all that. But this Lucy, she turned out to be really ordinary looking, you wouldn't look at her twice. I couldn't understand it at first, and then I realized what they're like together, her and my dad. They're like teenagers, holding hands; they really love each other. And after a bit I didn't think she was ordinary at all."

Melanie watched him steadily, betraying none of her surprise at Chris's sudden wish to confide in her; it was, she knew, a very sensitive area for him. "That's lovely for your Dad," she said when he appeared to have finished. She almost said, "He was wasted on your mum," but stopped just in time, realizing that that might be going too far.

Chris was about to say more, but at that point the sun emerged from behind a cloud with dramatic suddenness, and the piled white clouds in the distance were splashed with fire, as if liquid gold had been tipped over them in a magnificently lavish gesture. "Look at that!" Melanie cried, leaping up. "Imagine jumping into a sky like that!"

Someone was waving at them from the barn, shouting "Action stations!"

"Come on!" Chris grabbed Melanie's hand and they ran back to join the others.

"We're going up first, to see what the conditions are like," Mike told them. "We're going to do free-fall from five thousand feet. If that's okay, you can go up next."

Peter had already gone to fetch the plane, to taxi down the runway. A second instructor, Eddie, had arrived, and was helping Mike to sort out parachute packs and reserve chutes.

"Look." Chris pointed at the blackboard, where Mike had chalked details of the four planned lifts. Melanie's eyes went straight to the fourth grouping, which read "J. Shirley, M. Moss, M. E. Bolton." Chris and Mr Scanlon were to go in Lift 3.

The four experienced parachutists had already gone, walking down the runway through the bluish-green wheat. Everyone else went outside to watch. Melanie, now that she knew she was really going to jump, was conscious of a numb, wobbly feeling in her legs, and butterflies looping the loop in her stomach.

The tiny plane taxied along, turned and paused at the end of the runway; its engine raced, and then it was hurtling forward, lifting off the ground and circling away. It looked tiny, inconsequential as an insect, the whine of its engines sounding no more powerful than a wasp's drone. It climbed higher, illuminated for a moment brilliant white against a grey cloud. Melanie saw the wind drift indicator, a weighted length of crepe paper, flutter away from the plane and drift downwards; she knew that Mike would watch it carefully to see how far it landed from the target, and from that he would calculate the correct exit point, allowing for the speed and direction of the wind. The plane circled and climbed still higher, and then a tiny figure dropped away from it and fell for an alarming distance before the chute serpentined out and opened. The first jumper, manoeuvering skilfully, landed on his feet, engulfed by the collapsing folds of fabric, and within a few minutes all four men were on the ground, gathering their parachutes in their arms and walking back to the building, joking and laughing.

It looked so easy, Melanie told herself. Nothing to it at all. Mike had told them that the parachutes were one hundred percent reliable. What could conceivably go wrong?

In the storeroom behind the main building, Eddie handed out overalls, boots and helmets to the students; then Mike fitted parachute packs, checking the fit and all the fastenings, then double-checking. Finally, the three who were to jump next were given reserve chutes and small radio receivers, which were fastened to their fronts. Eddie went to his position by the wind-sock, where he would watch and give radio instructions to descending jumpers, if necessary.

The plane climbed for the static-line jumps. As Melanie heard the engine cut for the first exit, she went through the instructions in her mind: EXIT – plant both hands on the door frame, right foot out on the step. Above her, a body fell away from the plane, and the chute snaked out and opened.

"That's the hard part done," Mr Scanlon said. "I bet it seems like a million years before that chute opens, when you're up there."

It was all done very briskly and efficiently. Within a matter of minutes, the plane was on the ground, and the three students, smiling radiantly and all talking at once, were back at the building. Mr Scanlon and Chris, looking suddenly grim, were given reserve chutes and radios.

"Back soon," Chris said drily as Mike took them down to the plane.

Melanie waited on the tarmac with Jon. "This waiting really gets to you, doesn't it?" she remarked.

Her hands, thrust into the pockets of the overall, were sweating and at the same time icy cold, her legs so wobbly that it was amazing she was still upright. "I know what a cold sweat is now."

Jon didn't look as if he could trust himself to speak, his eyes fixed on the tiny plane as it took off and circled above.

Mr Scanlon was second to jump, recognizable by the white overalls he'd been given. There was no doubt that he'd be able to do it, Melanie thought; he hadn't even seemed nervous, for all his jokes. He seemed to have his canopy well under control, turning and judging his landing with impressive competence. Now it was Chris's turn. She watched anxiously as the indefinable shape dropped away, the chute flickered out and filled, and Chris was visible as a doll-like figure with legs waving slightly. Melanie was filled with pride in him, watching as he drifted down into his landing, crumpled, and disentangled himself from his chute; she'd known he'd do it, Chris could do anything, but all the same she felt like running across the field and hugging him, if it weren't for the horrible feeling of approaching doom. The plane was coming in to land, nose lowered.

"Now us."

Those who had jumped already were filled with elation, swapping stories and offering advice: "It was fantastic! You'll love it, you really will," and "I completely forgot to count. It went straight out of my head," and "That slipstream really hits you . . ."

Jon and Melanie were fitted with their reserve parachutes and radios, and Mike checked their pack and harness thoroughly. The packs were heavy, and Jon felt like a trussed-up chicken when all his harness straps had been tightened. He heard his voice saying, "Yes, thank you," as if from a distance, when Mike asked him if he was ready. He made himself walk down to the plane, although he felt more like running and hiding in the woods. Peter gave an encouraging grin as they reached the plane. "It's lovely up there. You could do with sunglasses."

Mike made them practise climbing out of the plane on to the step and jumping off a few times, and then they got in ready for take-off. Melanie got in first, Jon last, as he was Number One; Mike fastened their static lines to the strongpoint, showing them that they were firmly attached. They all had to get as far forward as possible in the cockpit, to take the weight off the tail during take-off. Jon was right up against the wind-screen, watching Peter's capable hands on the controls. Peter seemed very matter-of-fact, as if he were doing nothing more demanding than driving a milk-float; he cruised slowly to the end of the runway and prepared for take-off. The engines screamed as if in protest, and then they were launching forward, jolting on the rough runway, swaying in a sudden gust. Jon felt his stomach lurch as the plane lifted, and the airfield dropped away, the farm like a child's model with cows in the fields.

Jon crouched, rigid with fear, as the plane climbed

laboriously, buffeted by the wind and giving him a horrible feeling that it would stall and plummet back to earth. He'd only been on two passenger flights in his life, and both times during take-off he'd felt the same terror he was feeling now, a longing to get his feet back on the firm ground which was dropping further and further away beneath him. The sun was setting now, the underneath of the clouds tinged with a rosy pink, the distant fields hazy, spreading out in a patchwork of many-coloured greens and browns, but Jon was in no mood to admire the subtlety of the colours. It could be only minutes now before he would have to get out on to that tiny step, and cling there somehow until the dreaded command came. Peter spoke a few times into his radio microphone, his words inaudible. The plane banked alarmingly as it turned; Jon swayed with the movement, trying not to look out, but his head reeling at the thought that any moment now he was going to have to get out on to the step. The prospect seemed horrifying now; the practising on the ground had given him no idea what it would be like, up in the sky in this fragile-seeming craft. Jon forced himself to keep calm, going through the instructions in his mind. He knew he had to jump; not to would mean feebly going down in the plane, publicly admitting defeat. Mike's hand was on his shoulder, seemingly to offer reassurance, but also in readiness to give him the exit command.

"I'm going to open the door now," Mike shouted into his ear.

There was the predicted rush of slipstream; Jon, avoiding looking out, had hardly time to be alarmed before Mike shouted "CUT!" This was it. Jon felt sick, wondering if his limbs would obey his commands. He heard the engine noise lessen and then the brisk command "EXIT!" He had to look out now, shuffling backwards to get in line with the door, grasping his hands on the sides of the door frame as he'd been shown, thumbs inwards, and then putting his right foot out. The wind tore into him, snatching his leg and jerking it away from the step. He tried again, planting his foot down solidly, allowing for the force of the wind.

"Good lad!" He heard Mike's shouted words whirl away on the slipstream.

Now the worst part – grabbing the strut with one hand, climbing out, the wind buffeting him and making his eyes stream with tears. He remembered to get his weight down low, clinging to the strut with both hands, applying his whole mind to mastering his hands and feet, blacking out thoughts of what was to come, refusing to give way to the terror that threatened to overcome him. Somehow, he was there, leaning over the strut, one leg stretched out behind him, toe pointed – what was he doing, ballet dancing in the sky? – and then Mike shouted "*GO!*"

Jon hesitated for a moment and then pushed off with both hands. It was almost a relief to do so. He knew in that split second that his fear of chickening out had been greater than his fear of jumping.

* * *

Melanie looked at the horrible empty space where Jon
had been. God, she'd felt for him in the last few
minutes, knowing how he felt, but now she would need
all her sympathy for herself. Mike grinned at her and
gave her a thumbs-up signal to tell her that Jon was
all right, gesturing at her to move forward into the
Number One position next to Peter. She did so,
remembering to put her hand over the release pin for
her reserve chute, so that it couldn't be inflated
accidentally. She crouched there, noticing incon-
sequentially that Peter was wearing red-and-grey
checked socks, visible above his leather boots. Her
father had a pair just the same. It seemed very
important for the moment to concentrate on those
socks.

The plane had by now almost completed its circuit.
She tried to control her breathing, telling herself that
nothing could possibly go wrong. She heard the engine
noise cutting, and then "EXIT!", the word which
triggered off her trained responses. God, it was
terrifying, making yourself step out of the plane into
that vicious slipstream when every instinct screamed
at you to stay on board, to lie flat on the floor and
beg them to let you return to the ground . . . She felt
as insubstantial as an autumn leaf clinging to a twig.
She tried not to look down, willing herself to control
her panic, and to put all her trust in Mike and the
parachute.

"GO!"

She pushed off, barely hesitating. Her senses reeled; the fields and the sky were all jumbled up. She remembered to shout "one thousand, two thousand – " then there was a great jolt, the "friendly jerk" Mike had told them to expect. It was as if she had come round from an anaesthetic, waking up to find herself apparently quite motionless in the sky, held firmly by the harness and swaying slightly. She looked up. Never in her life had she seen such a beautiful sight as that glorious orange-and-white canopy, billowing with air, huge and strong, the taut lines going up from the risers like guy-ropes. She felt like shouting out with relief and exhilaration, into the sudden quiet after the engine noise. Whatever happened now, she'd done it – she'd jumped out of a plane at two thousand feet. She felt as light as thistledown, suspended above the twilit fields, which had darkened to soft shades of green and brown receding to smudged blue in the distance. The plane, as tiny as a buzzing insect, looked miles away. The sun was a glowing orange ball sinking to the horizon, the clouds soft pink deepening to violet, as if a celestial display had been arranged for her to admire while she hung there; it was a fantastic, unforgettable moment . . .

"Pull your left toggle," a crackly voice came eerily over her radio, a voice in the middle of the sky, and she remembered that she was supposed to be looking for the wind-sock and steering towards it. She'd forgotten all about the steering toggles. She looked up and found them, pulled hard on the left one, and turned away from the wind, feeling the swaying motion, seeing the airfield below her cut into triangular shapes by its runways, the wind-sock just visible. She gave her attention to the landing ahead, trying to gauge her speed and rate of descent. It was trickier than it had looked, the wind carrying her off her planned course, rotating the canopy. The ground already looked much closer; there was no time to admire the scenery now. Following her radio instructions, she turned back into the wind so that her landing would be slowed down. In spite of that, the ground was rushing up alarmingly now – it was true, what people said – and she tried to remember all she'd learned about landing: feet together and turned to one side, knees slightly bent, head bent forward . . .

She thought she'd got it right, but ended up winded with arms and legs sprawled, and a faceful of spring wheat and rich-smelling earth. The chute was still full of wind, dragging her with the gusts. She remembered to pull down on one of the risers and to unfasten one of the Capewell clips at her shoulder, to deflate the canopy. She felt sick with the impact of landing, but above all her spirits soared with exhilaration. She disentangled herself from the twisted lines and got to her feet, thinking of all the money they'd made.

Much later, Jon phoned Ruth.

"Jon, I'm awfully sorry," she burst out at once.

"Telling your parents. I didn't realize."

"Don't worry. I would have had to tell them anyway."

"I hope it didn't spoil it for you, arriving home."

"Well, perhaps; but at least it got it over with, them knowing already. I feel exhausted, facing the high jump twice in one day."

Eleven

Chris, calling round to see Melanie, found her in the restaurant kitchen surrounded by piles of coins, notes and cheques, the total proceeds of the Sponsored Fast.

She looked up, pleased to see him. "Hi! Let me get you something to drink, if you're staying for a minute. I could do with a break – this has taken me hours."

Chris sat down, looking at the various bits of paperwork spread out on the table. "Is this it?"

"For the Fast, yes. There's all the money from the parachute jump still to come."

"Did you see the local paper? Quite a write-up!"

"*Intrepid youngsters leap for famine relief?* Yes. And as a result of that, I got this letter this morning, forwarded from school." Melanie rummaged through her scattered papers, found the one she was looking for and waved it at Chris with an air of triumph.

"What is it?"

"You read it."

It was a letter, on an embossed sheet of thick paper bearing the name of a local department store.

"It's from Mr Baldwin of Baldwin's," Melanie

explained. "You know, the old boy who presented the prizes last prize day, and gave money to the school for the minibus and the computer centre."

"*Dear Miss Moss,*" Chris read. "*I have been most impressed by reports in the* Chronicle *of fund-raising efforts by you and fellow pupils, first the Sponsored Fast and then the parachute jump. You are obviously a young person after my own heart. I feel very proud to be associated with a school which produces such splendid efforts in the cause of famine relief.*

For this reason, I would be most honoured if you would allow me to donate a small sum of money as sponsorship. I propose to pay all the expenses for the parachute course, and also to give £5 for every person who participated in either event. If you would be kind enough to write back and let me know how much this will be, I shall be happy to send you a cheque.

With kind regards.

Yours very sincerely,

Reginald Baldwin."

Chris lowered the letter and looked at Melanie. "Crikey! That's an unexpected bonus. What a decent old chap!"

"It's terrific, isn't it?"

"Do you know what it comes to?"

"Yes." Melanie's mouth twitched with suppressed laughter. "Here's my working-out, look. The Fast has made £341.60, and thirty people took part in that, so thirty times five is a hundred and fifty pounds, bringing it up to £491.60. Then the parachute jump – " she turned to another sheet of paper " – would have made £470, but there were the course fees to take off, which would have brought it down to £310. Well, we can add the course fees back on again, plus five pounds each for the four of us who did it, which makes – " she waved a third sheet of paper at Chris – "four hundred and ninety pounds!"

Chris looked at the scrawled figures in disbelief, a grin spreading slowly across his face. "You mean to say – after all that arguing about which would bring in most, they both raised almost exactly the same?"

"Yes, isn't it great? But that's not all. If you add the two together, that makes £981.60 – just eighteen pounds something short of the thousand pounds I was aiming for."

"That's brilliant! Can't you ask old Baldwin to give you the extra eighteen?"

"No, we'll raise it ourselves."

She jumped up to fill the kettle for tea. Chris watched her quick, decisive movements, remembering what he'd come for. She pushed a strand of dark hair off her forehead with an impatient hand. Her face was excited, elated, her hazel eyes quick and intelligent.

"It means a lot to you, this fund-raising, doesn't it?" he asked her.

"Yes. I want to do it for a career. You sometimes see jobs advertised, for Oxfam or War on Want. If I can't do that, I'll do Voluntary Service Overseas."

"It'll be good practice for you if you do get a fund-raising job, doing all this, organizing us all. By

144

the way, did Jon's parents get over the shock of him doing the jump without asking them?"

"Ruth said they were a bit annoyed about him forging the signature, but they were choked with pride all the same." Melanie was getting mugs out of a cupboard. "I think it's really good that Jon and Ruth have got together, don't you?"

"Yes. A bit of a surprise, but nice."

"You'll have to watch out Ruth doesn't beat you at chess. Jon's been teaching her."

'Well, if she gets anywhere near Jon's standard, she'll certainly beat me." Chris paused, wanting to steer the conversation a different way. "It was fantastic, wasn't it, the parachute jump? I'll always remember it."

"Me too." Melanie poured boiling water into the tea-pot and sat down to wait for the tea to brew, remembering the tension of that evening and how it had erupted into excitement afterwards, and how terrific the feeling of achievement had been. They'd all admitted to having been absolutely petrified, but for Chris it had been different, sparking off a new interest; he wanted to carry on, when he was older and could afford it, progressing to free-fall. He had achieved the coveted comment "GATW" – Good All The Way – on his jump critique, whereas the others had been solely concerned with getting down in one piece, rather than with demonstrating any sort of style.

"You know," Chris said, "when we first talked

about the fund-raising, I wanted to do something tough and macho – do you remember?"

"Of course I do."

"Well, it's different now. The parachuting needed a different kind of toughness. I mean, look at Shirley. No-one would call him tough and brave, would they? But he did that jump, even though he was petrified. And you did it. It's the sort of toughness that means you make up your mind to do something, and you do it. It's to do with determination, really." He wanted to say, "and I admire you for that," but the words stuck in his throat. For some reason he felt shy with Melanie, remembering the conversation they'd had on the airfield. It was a feeling that was quite new to him. He usually treated girls with casual indifference.

"Sheer pig-headedness, my mum calls it in my case." She smiled at him across the table.

"It's a good quality, whatever you want to call it."

"You're just as pig-headed yourself, most of the time. What do you think we could do to get this extra eighteen pounds?" She'd picked up one of her account sheets again. "Hold a cake sale, or something? Though that's not very appropriate, is it, for famine relief."

Chris thought for a moment. "I know," he said after a moment. "We'll wash cars – Gary and me. Gary hasn't done anything yet. As soon as we get back to school, the two of us can wash teachers' cars, a pound a go."

"Good idea! Thanks. I'll join in too."

Melanie poured out the tea and passed him a mug.

Chris sipped it, wondering why he kept putting off what he wanted to ask her. He wasn't sure how to put it to her, afraid that she'd misunderstand, or laugh. He'd have to get round to it soon, or she'd be counting money again or planning new fund-raising ventures.

"Look, Melanie," he began. "I was wondering – are you going to be doing anything on Saturday night?"

She was on her feet again, looking for something. "Waitressing, I expect. I usually do on Saturdays. There's some biscuits somewhere – "

Chris felt like telling her to sit down and listen. "Well, what about Friday then?"

"I might be in the restaurant then as well, as it's the holidays. I can't remember."

"Well, if you're not, or some other time when you're not . . ." Chris began.

At that point the door opened and Melanie's mother came in holding a vast sheaf of pink and white carnations.

"Hello, Chris love! Sorry to rush you, but do you know what the time is, Melanie? It's time we got the tables laid and these flowers done, and you'll have to scrub down that table thoroughly if you've been counting money on it."

Melanie had noticed that the name Dunne appeared in the bookings diary for that evening – a table for two. She had wondered whether it might be Chris's mum with her latest boyfriend. Now, she did a

147

double-take when a dark, bearded man came in, accompanied by a small woman in a floral print dress.

"I'll serve these two," she told her mother. "It's Chris's Dad, and I haven't seen him for ages."

She went to show them to their table. "Hello, Mr Dunne! How are you?"

"Melanie! Nice to see you. I gather you're quite a local celebrity these days! This is Melanie, a good friend of Chris's," Jeff told the young woman. "Melanie, this is Lucy."

"Oh, you're the girl who organized the parachuting," Lucy said at once, shaking Melanie's hand. "It sounded very exciting. Chris has talked of nothing else since."

They asked her a lot of questions about the parachute jump. Melanie studied Lucy carefully, remembering what Chris had said about her. Lucy's dress looked crisp and carefully pressed, and she looked as if she felt self-conscious in it, as if she wasn't used to wearing a dress. She reminded Melanie of a small girl dressed up for a party; she had a lively, animated expression which made her look very youthful. Melanie, leaving them to study their menus while she took their order for drinks, thought she looked nice, a good match for Chris's dad. She couldn't help looking across at them as she hurried to and fro, noticing that they both looked lit up with happiness, holding hands across the table, their heads close together in the candle's soft glow, as if they were sharing some delightful secret. Their happiness both

148

attracted and excluded her, making her feel oddly and uncharacteristically subdued.

"Onion soup for two, please, and whitebait for one, followed by Steak Tartare . . ."

Melanie heard what the elderly man was saying, and her pen wrote it down, but her mind wasn't on the job. She found herself thinking about Chris, about the way he seemed to have changed recently, becoming more serious and thoughtful, perhaps because of what had happened to his dad. He seemed less anxious to keep up his laid-back image, more willing to show his sensitive side. Melanie knew that the last two years had been difficult for him; he'd rarely talked about it, but she knew that his parents' separation had hit him hard. She knew how much he loved his father, in his undemonstrative way.

She returned to the kitchen and relayed her orders.

"Okay, love. Here's the drinks for Chris's dad. Is that his girlfriend with him?"

She delivered the drinks. Jeff looked up at her with a grin so Chris-like that it sent a sudden stab through her. She took the order, and walked away in a daze. She'd never openly acknowledged it to herself, but now saw it with clarity, that she wanted more from her relationship with Chris than just friendship. He was a friend, but more than that, someone she'd always admired and felt drawn to, even through his brooding silences or his periods of brash extroversion. If only he wasn't so *gorgeous* – it was partly because of that, and partly because his tastes so obviously ran to similarly-endowed females like Lisa, that Melanie had kept herself in the background, realizing, if she'd thought about it at all, that Chris would never think of her in that sort of way. But, she recalled, drifting across the restaurant with a tray of soup, hadn't he been trying to change things between them, trying to put their relationship on a different footing? Only she'd been too busy to listen, waffling on about money and cake sales – she hadn't even let him finish what he was trying to say. The thought struck her forcibly, as she remembered Chris's unusual air of hesitation. God, she was thick! – unable to recognize something so blindingly obvious, now that she stopped to consider it. She could hardly stop herself from laughing out loud with delight. She felt like dumping the tray of soup in the lap of the nearest customer and rushing round to Chris's house straight away.

Chris was annoyed. He sprawled on the sofa, trying to read a book, but distracted by the stupid situation-comedy Ian and his mother were watching. His mother had just finished filing her nails and was now carefully applying nail-varnish. Her toe-nails were already painted in the same shade of scarlet. She must be going out again, Chris thought, watching her. You were in a bad way when your mother had a better social life than you did.

"I thought you said you were going round to

Melanie's?" she asked, blowing on her fingernails to dry them.

"I did. She was busy."

His frown deepened as he remembered his brief visit. Melanie was infuriating, he thought, always dominating the conversation, rushing off on some new topic whenever he wanted to get a word in. He'd decided to wait until the next day, but now he suddenly threw his book down and went out into the hall. He'd phone her now, restaurant or no restaurant, and she'd have to listen whether she liked it or not. If he wanted to ask her out, then he damn well would ask her out.

"I'm sorry, I think you've made a mistake – we ordered steak, not chicken."

Melanie looked around wildly. Someone else was trying to attract her attention. "Excuse me, miss, I think you've given us the wrong starters. I did try to tell you . . ."

She looked down at her notepad, the words and numbers making no sense to her. Her mother swept in, noticing the concerned faces of customers.

"What's the problem?"

"Sorry, I've muddled everything up. Who ordered chicken?" She snatched the offending plate away.

"We've ordered chicken," Jeff said, "but you've given us Baked Alaska." Melanie registered that he looked amused by the confusion, unaware that his

151

own son was indirectly responsible for her fuddled mental state.

Mrs Moss was shuffling plates briskly, darting from one table to another, apologizing to the customers. "The Baked Alaska's over here. Onion soup for Table Four." She gave Melanie a puzzled glance. "Are you all right, love?"

"Fine, thanks. I'm sorry." Melanie tried to regain her composure. What on earth had she been thinking of? She went back to the kitchen with her empty tray.

Paul was talking on the telephone, his back to her. He turned as she came in.

"It's for you."

Melanie hurried across to the phone. "Is it . . . ?"

"He didn't say his name."

She took the receiver from him, her hand not quite steady. "Hello?"

"Hello, Melanie – it's me, Chris . . ."

Paul was looking at her curiously. She felt a stupid, idiotic grin spreading all over her face. "I know," she said.

With grateful thanks to Mike Bolton and Peter Styles of the Oxon and Northants Parachute Club, for making me jump.

Hairline Cracks
John Robert Taylor

Sam Lydney's mother knows too much. She has realized that a public inquiry into the safety of a local nuclear power station has been rigged and, despite his father's assurances, Sam is certain she's been kidnapped. He can trust no one except his resourceful friend Mo. They must work alone to piece together the clues and discover who has taken his mother and where she may be kept.

An Armada Original

On the Spot
Mark Daniel

Ben O'Connell has a problem. He is small. Humiliated at home and bullied at school, he seems a born loser. But Ben has a special talent for snooker and he's determined to reach the top.

It seems that no one can beat him and nothing will stand in his way – until scheming Perry Curling becomes his manager. To him, a boy like Ben is made for hustling round seedy snooker joints. Winning championships, says Curling, is the stuff dreams are made of. After all, this is tough '80s Merseyside.

But Ben is aiming for the top . . .

An Armada Original

The
Sin Bin
series

KEITH MILES

1	Iggy	£1.95	☐
2	Melanie	£1.95	☐
3	Tariq	£1.95	☐
4	Bev	£1.95	☐

The Headmaster of Woodfield Comprehensive School cannot cope with troublemakers – so he sends them to the Sin Bin, a special annexe where all privileges are suspended and the pupils are under constant supervision. A spell in the Sin Bin was supposed to frighten pupils back into line, but instead it conferred on them a special status. They were heroes.

ARMADA

Stevie Day
Series
JACQUELINE WILSON

Supersleuth	£2.25	☐
Lonely Hearts	£2.25	☐
Rat Race	£2.25	☐
Vampire	£2.25	☐

An original new series featuring an unlikely but irresistible heroine – fourteen-year-old Stevie Day, a small skinny feminist who has a good eye for detail which, combined with a wild imagination, helps her solve mysteries.

"Jacqueline Wilson is a skilful writer, readers of ten and over will find the (Stevie Day) books good, light-hearted entertainment."

Children's Books December 1987

"Sparky Stevie"   *T.E.S. January 1988*

ARMADA

The Pit

ANN CHEETHAM

The summer has hardly begun when Oliver Wright is plunged into a terrifying darkness. Gripped by fear when workman Ted Hoskins is reduced to a quivering child at a demolition site, Oliver believes something of immense power has been disturbed. But what?

Caught between two worlds – the confused present and the tragic past – Oliver is forced to let events take over.

£1.95 ☐

Nightmare Park

LINDA HOY

A highly original and atmospheric thriller set around a huge modern theme park, a theme park where teenagers suddenly start to disappear . . .

£1.95 ☐

ARMADA

All these books are available at your local bookshop or newsagent, or can be ordered from the publisher. To order direct from the publishers just tick the title you want and fill in the form below:

Name _____

Address _____

_____

Send to: Collins Childrens Cash Sales
            PO Box 11
            Falmouth
            Cornwall
            TR10 9EN

Please enclose a cheque or postal order or debit my Visa/ Access –

   Credit card no:

   Expiry date:

   Signature:

– to the value of the cover price plus:

UK: 60p for the first book, 25p for the second book, plus 15p per copy for each additional book ordered to a maximum charge of £1.90.

BFPO: 60p for the first book, 25p for the second book plus 15p per copy for the next 7 books, thereafter 9p per book.

Overseas and Eire: £1.25 for the first book, 75p for the second book. Thereafter 28p per book.

Armada reserve the right to show new retail prices on covers which may differ from those previously advertised in the text or elsewhere.

ARMADA

RUN

WITH
THE
HARE

LINDA NEWBERY

Elaine has to decide whether to run with the hare or hunt with the hounds – is she really committed to Animal Rights or is she more interested in Mark?

"It is a genuine novel, setting its interests within a satisfying context of teenage relationships and activities. The book is a good story, an intelligent argument . . ." *The Times Literary Supplement*

"Elaine is an intelligent and sensible heroine and by setting the romance in the world of Animal Rights, the author focuses attention on the adult world which appears confusing and often unfeelingly harsh to young people." *The School Librarian*